Dead Angels
(Kiera Hudson Series Two)
Book 2

Tim O'Rourke

ISBN: 10:1478377364
ISBN-13:978-1478377368

Story Editor
Lynda O'Rourke
Book cover designed by:
Tom O'Rourke
Copyright: Tom O'Rourke 2011
Edited by:
Carolyn M. Pinard
carolynpinardconsults@gmail.com
www.thesupernaturalbookeditor.com
Series Logo Designed by
Suzi Midnight

For Jane Evans
You know why...

More books by Tim O'Rourke

Vampire Shift (Kiera Hudson Series 1) Book 1
Vampire Wake (Kiera Hudson Series 1) Book 2
Vampire Hunt (Kiera Hudson Series 1) Book 3
Vampire Breed (Kiera Hudson Series 1) Book 4
Wolf House (Kiera Hudson Series 1) Book 4.5
Vampire Hollows (Kiera Hudson Series 1) Book 5
Dead Flesh (Kiera Hudson Series 2) Book 1
Dead Night (Kiera Hudson Series 2) Book 1.5
Dead Angels (Kiera Hudson Series 2) Book 2
Cowgirls & Vampires (Samantha Carter Series) Book 1
Black Hill Farm (Book 1)
Black Hill Farm: Andy's Diary (Book 2)
Doorways (Book 1)

You can contact Tim O'Rourke at
www.Ravenwoodgreys.com
Or by email at Ravenwoodgreys@aol.com

Chapter One

Kiera

"What did he do to me?" I shouted at Potter.

"He killed you!" Potter said back, coming towards me from the other side of the table.

The windows in the consulting room rattled in their frames, as a steady wind blew hard outside.

"I know he killed me!" I snapped as he gripped my upper arms. I wasn't mad at Potter, I was mad at the thought of not knowing what Jack Seth had done to me before he had killed me. So many times I had looked into the killer's eyes and seen myself with him. I had watched as he had hurt me, paralysed me through fear or lust, so I couldn't fight him off.

"He's full of shit," Potter tried to calm me.

"Whatever he did to me, Seth said that I loved every moment of it," I reminded him, and the nightmarish images of Seth and me together that raced across my mind made me feel sick and violated.

Potter looked at Isidor and Kayla, who still sat around the table watching us, and hooked his thumb toward the door.

Knowing what he meant, Kayla pushed her chair back, stood up, and said, "I'm gonna go check on Sam." Then, fixing Isidor with a hard stare, she added, "Isidor, let's go and see if Sam is feeling any better."

"Okay, sure," Isidor said, and both of them left the room.

Once on our own, Potter looked into my eyes and said, "Don't let Seth put you in a mind-fuck. That's what he wants."

"But he said that he seduced that pathologist into telling him my name," I reminded him over the wind that was now beginning to pick up outside. Hearing this, Potter appeared to flinch in my arms. "Are you okay?" I asked.

Potter loosened his hold on me and stepped back towards the table. "I'm fine," he said, taking a cigarette from his pocket and lighting it.

"What's wrong?" I quizzed, suspecting that he was hiding something from me.

"Honest, I'm okay," he said, breaking my stare and going to the window where he peered up into the night sky. "It looks like a storm is coming."

"When have you ever given a crap about the weather?" I asked him, sensing that something wasn't right. "What aren't you telling me?"

"There's nothing to tell, sweet-cheeks," he said with his back to me and a cloud of blue smoke forming around his head.

Striding across the room, I went to join him at the window. "Don't shut me out, Potter. What do you know?"

"Nothing," he sighed, glancing at me, the cigarette dangling from the corner of his mouth.

"You're lying," I whispered, starting to feel nervous, yet I didn't know why. "Talk to me, Potter."

"I can't," he whispered back, staring out of the window.

It was so dark outside that I could see his reflection looking back at me, and I could see that his eyes looked darker than usual.

"You can't, or you won't?" I pushed, placing my hand gently on his muscular forearm.

"You're just gonna have to trust me," he said to the window.

"You're scaring me," I whispered, and I did feel scared. I was scared of what Seth might have done to me before tearing me to pieces. Did Potter know something about that? But how would he? We'd been together since coming back from the dead. No, Potter had left that day, the day he had gone to get my police badge and that picture of me and my dad.

"You have nothing to be scared of," he said, finally turning to face me. The look of sadness on his face frightened me more than anything. The last time I had seen such sorrow in his eyes was when he'd cradled Murphy's dead body in his arms beneath the Fountain of Souls.

"Is it Murphy?" I asked him, my voice barely a whisper as I looked into his eyes.

"Murphy?" he frowned, his eyes growing wide.

"I know you miss him," I said. "I know it's him you are thinking of when you sit and chain smoke in front of the fireplace. He was like a father to you – he was like a father to all of us. I wish he was here, too. I wish my father..."

"Stop," Potter said, raising his hand, and turning away. "I can't talk about this anymore."

"Why not?" I asked, pulling him back so I could look into his eyes.

Potter stared down at me, and with a grim and troubled look on his face, he said, "Kiera, I can't talk about this right now." Then, leaning in close, he planted the softest of kisses on my mouth.

"You know you can tell me anything," I whispered, brushing my cheek against his.

"Not everything," he whispered back.

Before I had the chance to ask what he meant by that, I heard Kayla scream.

Chapter Two

Isidor

I followed my sister from the study, and closed the door behind me. Potter wanted to be alone with Kiera and that was cool with me. They had stuff they needed to talk about, and I'd probably say the wrong thing if I stayed. Potter would have gotten all cranky with me again, and I didn't have to do too much for that to happen.

I knew that Potter thought I was thick – a joke. Maybe I did get things wrong at times but I wasn't like him. I hadn't lived above ground as long as he had. He knew more about life above ground than me – that was a given. But I knew stuff too – I had seen things – and I wasn't just talking about episodes of "Scooby-Doo."

While Potter had been away, I'd tried to bring myself up to speed by checking the Internet for some of the stuff that Potter had talked about. I did it to keep up with him, like any younger brother who looks up to the elder one. But there seemed to be so much to learn about this strange world. And it was *strange.* It was strange way before it got *pushed.*

There was that word again. *Pushed.*

Push. I had seen that word before. But I had never suspected its significance until Kiera had written it down on that advert which Kayla and I had posted in the shop window. I had wanted to say something – I wanted to say that I had seen that word before – but would anyone have listened to me? Would I have been taken seriously? Not by Potter, that was for sure. He would have just ribbed me and told me I was talking shit again.

But I had kept quiet before and it had cost me my life – it had cost my sister's life. Back then, as we had crossed The Hollows, I felt that I was unable to say anything. I was scared that the others would have dismissed me – or worse, laughed at me. And could I have blamed them? Even when I was sure that Luke was really Elias Munn, I felt unable to tell my friends what I feared. I hadn't even been able to tell Kayla. I didn't think twice about killing a werewolf if I had to, I didn't hesitate drawing my crossbow in defence, but I was so often scared of saying what I felt for fear of...fear of what, exactly?

In my heart, I knew what I was scared of – I was scared of getting hurt. I'd been there before and didn't want to go back. For such a tall guy, with jet black hair and even darker tattoos up my arm and neck, the goatee beard and eyebrow piercing, I was too soft, I guess. I looked confident –but I wasn't. The tattoos and stuff were there because they had to be – not because I had wanted them. Before the black flames, which covered my arm and licked up beneath my chin, I had been different. To wear them was like wearing a mask – but who was I wearing that mask for, and why? I had an idea, but would anyone listen to me?

I followed Kayla into the great hall to find the large double front doors ajar. Some of the leaves that Potter had raked into a pile on the drive now blew through the gap and circled around the hall. Guessing that Jack Seth, the boy with the burns, and Emily Clarke had left the door open on their way out, I closed it against the wind that chilled the hallway. It had been a real shame to discover that Ms. Clarke had been mixed up with Seth, as she had seemed real nice. The Oompa-Loompa (I'd have to Toogle that) with the burns, as Potter had called him, looked kinda freaky, a perfect match for Seth, I thought. But Seth had tricked us all, and now the world – this new pushed one, was gonna change.

The Treaty that the wolves and humans had lived by was now in tatters, and even though it wasn't our fault, we would be blamed for it; Seth would make sure of that. He had set us all up good and proper. How long would it take for the wolves to figure out what we had done at Ravenwood School? I didn't know, but I could guess it wouldn't take long before they came in search of us. Where would we run to this time? There were no more Hollows – we were trapped here?

Kiera would figure it out – she always figured everything out. But maybe I could help this time around. Perhaps I should tell her about that word *push* and where I had seen it before. But knowing that Potter would probably only take the piss if I told Kiera my story, I thought I would keep it to myself just a little while longer.

"Are you coming or what, Isidor?" Kayla asked, wrenching me from my thoughts.

I turned away from the front door and looked at her standing at the foot of the wide staircase. Her red hair looked as if it were on fire as it glimmered in the soft light coming from the chandelier above us.

"Coming where?" I asked her, crossing the hall.

"To check on Sam," she said, her eyes sparkling with that twinkle which had been there ever since she had returned from Ravenwood. I knew that Sam had put that sparkle in her eyes – she liked him. I was glad for her, but kinda sad, too. It was nice to see her happy for once. Since returning from The Hollows, I'd known that Kayla hadn't been happy. She'd seemed haunted somehow. I'd seen it in her eyes and heard it in her sobs, which had echoed through the manor at night. Now I saw something different in her eyes – it was an eagerness for life again and a desire for Sam to get well. That's what made me sad for her. Since returning from Ravenwood School, Sam had been ill. Night after night and day after day, Kayla had sat beside his bed, wiping the fever from his brow, and cooling his burning body with a damp sponge and towels.

"What do you think is wrong with him?" I had asked her one night, as she had sat beside Sam's bed, one of her hands folded over his.

"I think it has something to do with what happened back at the chapel," she hushed, fearful that she might wake the boy.

"The matching?" I whispered back, looking at the sallow colour of Sam's flesh. It had a sickly yellow tinge to it, and was coated in a thin sheen of sweat.

"I guess," she said, looking up at me. "You saw how his face seemed to get sucked into that wolf's. It was trying to match with him. Take his soul."

"But it didn't happen – we stopped it," I tried to convince myself more than her.

"Maybe we only half stopped it?" she mumbled, as if scared to say the words out loud for fear of it being the truth.

"What's that s'posed to mean?" I asked, kneeling down beside the bed and handing her a wet towel.

Kayla took it from me, and as she dabbed it against his chest, I could see what looked like waves of steam seeping from his skin. "What if the wolf has infected him somehow? I mean, look at his face."

In the pale light from the bedside lamp, I peered at Sam. His face looked swollen, as if he had been badly beaten. His eyes were swollen shut, the skin around them purple and bruised-looking. His nostrils were red and sore, and snot ran from them in thick streams. With each laboured breath he took, Sam's throat and chest made a hideous rattling noise, like he had swallowed a child's toy. Sam's lips were blistered and puckered. As I looked upon his grotesque face, I realised how much Kayla musta cared for Sam. Most girls would have been too repulsed to even look at him, let alone sit in the semi-darkness throughout the night and mop the fever from his brow.

"We should get him to a hospital," I told her.

"Potter says no," she said, her eyes fearful.

"Why not?" I asked, frowning.

"He reckons it will draw unwanted attention," she started to explain in such a tone that I knew she wasn't convinced by what Potter had suggested. "The police might start asking questions as to how he came by his injuries, who we are..."

"Couldn't we just drive him to the hospital and leave him...?" I started.

"No way," Kayla snapped. "I promised Sam I wouldn't leave him. "Besides, he knows what I am – what we all are.

Potter's worried that in his delirious state he might talk about what he saw – what he witnessed us do back at the school."

"We can't just sit back and watch him die," I told her, the steam curling up from his body.

"He won't die," Kayla insisted. "I'm going to take care of him."

But I hadn't been so sure, and as I now followed Kayla through the dim narrow passageways towards Sam's room, I was fearful of what we might find.

Chapter Three

Isidor

Kayla pushed Sam's bedroom door open. The room was dimly lit, and being so high up in the manor, the wind blew around the eaves, sounding like a child crying as they woke from a nightmare. The bedroom window was open, and the curtains billowed out like two sails in the cold night air. Then, way off in the distance, I heard the rumble of thunder.

Sam lay on his bed in the far corner of the room, and even though it was bitterly cold, tendrils of steam coiled up from his body and leaked from his mouth and nostrils. He writhed about on the sheets, which were damp and clung to his body.

"Sam," Kayla gasped as she crossed the room towards him, the heels of her boots echoing back from the bare wooden floorboards.

The boy made a growling sound in the pit of his throat, as thick lengths of ropey snot sprayed from between his lips and spattered the wall in black strips.

Kayla took him by the shoulders as if to restrain him, but his skin was so hot that she snapped her hands away.

"What's happening to him?" she cried.

Then, from the corner of my eye, I saw something move in the shadows that darkened the other side of the room.

"Who's there?" I called out, believing that I had seen someone hiding from us.

Sam cried out again, and this time he sounded like he was being strangled. I spun around to look at him, and as I did, I heard the sound of running from behind me. Glancing back over my shoulder, I caught just the briefest glimpse of what looked like someone sneaking out of the room and disappearing onto the landing.

"Who's there?" I called out again, bolting towards the bedroom door. Believing that it might be Jack Seth, suddenly fearing that perhaps he hadn't left the manor after all, I wished that I'd had my crossbow with me. With my claws springing from my fists, I peered left, then right, along the landing. There, just at the foot of the stairs, I saw the figure again. Almost covered completely by shadow, its skin looked grey – chalky like – and cracked.

A *statue?* I wondered.

"Hey!" I called after it.

The figure stopped, then peering back at me over its fractured-looking shoulder, it looked at me with its featureless face. Then, placing one broken finger over the area where its mouth should have been, it said,
"Shhhhhhhhhhhhhhhhhhhhhhhhhh!"

Then, moving with the speed of a Vampyrus, it rushed away down the stairs. I raced down the landing after it, but before I'd even reached the top of the stairs, Kayla began to scream from behind me. Not knowing whether I should continue after the statue or head back to the bedroom, I hesitated.

"Oh shit," I sighed aloud in the gloom, as I heard the sound of the statue's footsteps fade away down the steps. Knowing in my heart that I had to go back for Kayla, I spun around and headed back in the direction of the way I had come.

"Did you see that?" I gasped as I raced back into the room.

"Have you seen this?" Kayla screeched.

Sam was kneeling on all fours on the bed. His arms and legs were locked rigid, his spine a series of white lumps glowing through the flesh that now seemed to stretch over his back. I took hold of Kayla's arm and yanked her back, away from the bed.

"We've got to help him, Isidor!" she screamed.

"I don't think we can," I said, pulling her tight against me.

Sam dropped onto the mattress, where he rolled onto his back. He opened his mouth and released a series of painful sounding howls. His cracked lips started to bleed as they began to tear. Then, throwing his arms up into the air, we stood and watched as Sam's fingers began to stretch and elongate. Turning his head in our direction, Sam snapped open his eyes and looked at us. They shone a bright yellow, and lit up the room.

"*Help me*," he pleaded and clutched at the air with the claws that had now formed at the end of each of his wrists. It was the first time that I'd heard Sam speak since we had brought him to the manor, and his voice sounded deep, as if he were gargling on a throat full of gravel.

"Does he always sound like that?" I asked Kayla.

"No, Isidor," she whispered, her own voice sounding confused and lost.

Then, over the sound of the approaching thunder and the roar of the wind, Sam began to howl as his whole body seemed to stretch and twist out of shape. His feet began to grow, each toe capped with an ivory-looking nail. Sam's pyjama bottoms began to tear as his calf and thigh muscles rippled beneath the material.

A 'V' shape of fur broke out down the front of his chest and glistened in the glow of the lamp. Thick lengths of fur bristled down each of his meaty forearms, and thinned over the back of his new claws. Then, Sam's face began to change shape. His nose grew longer taking on the shape of a snout. His ears stretched into points on either side of his face, and black hair grew from beneath his chin, giving him a beard that even I would have been proud of.

Once the transformation had taken place, Sam collapsed onto his side and lay panting like a tired dog on a hot summer's day. He looked at us, and Kayla began to sob. Sam didn't look like a wolf, but then again, he didn't look like a teenage boy anymore – he looked half and half. He looked half boy and half wolf – a half breed – and if he survived, I understood the torment that he would go through. Maybe that's why Kayla stood sobbing in my arms. Not because she feared him, but because she knew that living the life of a half-breed was a hard one. It was a curse.

Then, in a voice that sounded as if it was consumed with pain, Sam stared at us with his burning eyes and said, "Kayla, help me. Please."

"How?" she whispered.

"Take me to the Fountain of Souls," he pleaded.

Chapter Four

Kiera

Potter reached Sam's bedroom just before me. With his long legs, he had climbed the stairs two at a time. As he charged at them, I saw his claws shoot from his fingertips. Halfway up the stairs, the sound of howling echoed around the upper reaches of the manor, and with a flick of my wrists, my own claws sprang out.

Inside the room, Potter suddenly paused, and I had to pull up sharp to stop myself from clattering into him. He stood next to Kayla and Isidor who were rooted to the floor and staring down at the bed. I looked to see what had drawn their attention, and was shocked by what I saw peering up at us from the glow of the lamp. Sam lay on his side, but he didn't exactly look like Sam anymore. He had grown in size and two giant fur-covered feet hung over the end of the bed. His hands were huge claws, and his fingernails looked as sharp as a set of dinner knives. But it was his face. He looked half wolf and half boy. His eyes burnt a fierce yellow and they reminded me of Jack Seth's – they reminded me of the Skin-walkers.

Part of me feared him, but another part of me pitied him, as he lay on his side panting and howling in agony. I don't think Potter felt the same at all, as he lunged across the room at him.

"No!" Kayla screamed as she broke free of Isidor's arms and snatched at Potter.

"Let go of me!" Potter barked at her, tugging his arm free. "He's a wolf – a Skin-walker!"

"He's my friend," Kayla screeched at him.

"Not anymore," Potter snapped. "He's one of them."

"No he's not!" Kayla insisted. "Look at him. He hasn't changed properly. The matching was broken halfway through."

"And how do we know he won't change fully one night and kill us all in our sleep?" Potter tried to warn her.

17

"*Please!*" Sam howled, and his cry for help sounded as raw as the growing wind outside.

"See, the boy's begging me to kill him," Potter said, staring down at the half-wolf. "He wants me to end his suffering."

"No he doesn't," Kayla hissed, grabbing Potter's arm again, and turning him around so he had to look at her. "He wants us to take him to the Fountain of Souls."

"This just keeps getting better and better," Potter groaned. Then, staring hard at Kayla, he added, "Do I have to remind you what happened the last time we went there?"

"Murphy died," I whispered.

"Exactly!" Potter sighed. "Going back there is insane. How does the kid know about that place, anyhow?"

"Maybe he..." Isidor started.

"No one asked you," Potter cut over him. "I'll tell you how he knows, because the wolf living inside of him knows. That part of him wants us to go to the Fountain of Souls."

"Please help me," Sam howled again, closing his eyes in agony.

"I say we kill him," Potter said. "It would be the best thing for us, and for him."

"No!" Kayla shouted, scrambling between Potter and the bed. Holding out her arms, she added, "You'll have to kill me first."

"Kayla, if you think I'm taking the Michael J. Fox lookalike to the Fountain of Souls, you must be out of your freaking mind."

Then, stepping forward, Isidor peered over Potter's shoulder at Sam. "I guess he does look a little bit like a mouse," he said.

Frowning, Potter turned to look at Isidor and said, "What are you talking about?"

"Michael J. Fox," Isidor beamed. "Now I did Toogle him. He did the voice for that cute mouse, Stuart Little. And I can see what you mean; I guess Sam does look a little bit like Stuart Little, although his fur was white and..."

"I'm not talking about Stuart-*fucking*-Little you cretin," Potter cut over him. "When I say he looks like Michael J. Fox, I'm talking about Teen Wolf, for fuck's sake."

"Teen Wolf?" Isidor asked, sounding confused. "But I thought you said the wolf was called Michael Jackson, not Michael J. Fox?"

"Is this some kinda hobby of yours?" Potter asked, sounding exasperated.

"Hobby?" Isidor frowned. "I don't know what you mean?"

"I just can't believe you thought that when I referred to the wolf-boy lying over there as Michael J. Fox, you honestly thought I was suggesting he looked like a three-inch computer-generated fucking mouse! You can't be that thick."

"I did think it was a little odd," Isidor said thoughtfully as he looked down at Sam. "But he is covered in hair like Stuart Little, so I thought that's what you meant."

Throwing his arms up in the air, Potter cried, "I give up! I don't know if I can do this shit anymore."

"What shit?" Isidor asked, looking confused.

"Listening to the shit that comes out of your mouth..." Potter started.

"Enough already," I cut in. "This isn't going to get us anywhere."

"He gets on my nerves," Potter said, jabbing his thumb in Isidor's direction.

"And killing Sam isn't the answer," Isidor said in his own defence.

"It isn't Sam anymore," Potter wheeled on him.

"That still doesn't give you the right to decide on who lives and who dies," Isidor said, standing firm.

"If that thing lives, then we will die," Potter shouted, going toe to toe with Isidor.

Kayla cut in between them. "It is Sam. It's the wolf that tried to match with him that we can see..."

"Help me, please," the wolf-boy on the bed murmured.

Ignoring the others, I went to the side of the bed and looked down at him. "Who are you?"

19

"I'm Sam Brook," he whispered, his voice deep, yet soft. "I know you fear me, but I'm not going to harm you."

"How many times has a wolf told us that?" Potter reminded me.

"He won't hurt us," Kayla pleaded, standing at the foot of the bed where Sam's feet hung.

"He could turn on us at any moment," Potter told her.

"Until that happens, I don't think we have the right to kill him," Isidor said.

There was a pause as they looked at me for the answer. In that silence I could hear the sound of Sam's laboured breathing, the wind screaming outside, and the boom of fast approaching thunder. Looking at Potter, I eventually said, "Isidor is right. We can't kill Sam. We don't have the right – not until he becomes a threat at least."

"He's a wolf, Kiera, that makes him threat number one," Potter snapped back.

"Half wolf," Kayla said from the foot of the bed.

"I think we should help him," Isidor said, going to stand beside his sister.

Then, staring me straight in the eye, Potter said, "You're making a mistake. How many times has a wolf got to betray us before you learn we can't trust them?"

Potter's voice sounded cold, but I knew he wouldn't harm Sam – not yet, anyhow. But I felt Potter was wrong – I once knew a wolf that could be trusted. He had been a true friend and had died trying to help me.

"What about Nik?" I asked Potter.

"What about him?"

"He helped me – he was true to his word," I said.

"After years of killing," Potter said. "But what about the others? Eloisa, Sparky, and do I have to remind you of our dear friend, Jack Seth? Wolves can't be trusted."

"You can trust me," Sam suddenly murmured from the bed, where he lay curled in pain.

"I've heard that before," Potter hissed.

"And there were plenty of Vampyrus that deceived us too," I reminded him gently.

"Yeah, there was Taylor, Phillips, Mrs. Payne" Isidor said, counting them off on his fingers. "And need I mention Lu – "

"Okay, wise arse," Potter spoke before Isidor could finish. "But let's see how smart you are when the wolf-boy rips your head clean off." Then Potter was gone, striding out of the room.

"Mind the statue," Isidor called out.

"Fuck the statues," Potter shouted back over his shoulder.

"What statue?" I asked, staring at Isidor.

"I'm sure there was a statue in here with Sam," he told me.

"Where is it now?" I peered into the shadows of the corner of the room.

"It disappeared real quick down the landing when Kayla and I came in."

"I didn't pass it on the stairs," I said thoughtfully, as I wondered about the statues that suddenly kept reappearing and disappearing again.

"Why do you think we keep seeing them?" Kayla asked me.

But before I'd had the chance to answer, Sam howled in pain again and gripped his sides.

"We don't have time to worry about those statues now," I said, reaching out and touching Sam's arm. His skin was burning up and I pulled my hand away. "We need to get him some help, and fast."

"Are we going to take him to the Fountain of Souls?" Kayla asked.

"I guess," I breathed. Then, looking at Kayla and Isidor, I added, "Pack some stuff, we're leaving tonight."

Chapter Five

Kiera

"You know I think you're wrong about this," Potter said, as I threw a rucksack into the boot of the car. The bottles of Lot 13 hidden within it made a clinking sound.

"So why are you tagging along?" I half-smiled at him, cocking an eyebrow.

"You know why I'm coming along," he grunted. "Somebody's got to watch your back on these half-brained adventures you keep going on."

"Half-brained?" I said, the wind so fierce now that my hair blew back off my face and billowed out behind me.

"Well I don't call driving up into the mountains in search of the Fountain of Souls a smart idea. Murphy wouldn't have agreed to it," he said, throwing Kayla's and Isidor's rucksacks into the boot of the car.

"Murphy was the person who first took us there," I told him. "Besides, Murphy isn't here anymore. It's down to us to call the shots these days."

"I guess," he said thoughtfully.

"Are you sure you're okay?" I asked, narrowing my eyes at him.

"I'm fine," he shrugged. Then, changing the subject he looked back towards the manor and said, "Here come Kayla and Isidor with the *wolf*-boy."

I followed Potter's stare, and could see Kayla and Isidor hoisting Sam down the front steps of the manor. They carried him between them, Sam's arms draped around their shoulders. His head hung low, his chin nestled in the V-shaped strip of hair on his chest and long, clawed feet dragging behind him. Potter glanced at me and raised his eyebrows. He held open the boot, and as Isidor and Kayla came closer, he shifted the bags around inside.

"Put him in here," Potter said to them. "There's enough room."

"Sam's not going in the boot," Kayla gasped. "He might suffocate."

"He's not going to suffocate," Potter told her flatly. "Besides, he might start freaking out again and we could crash the car."

"He might die in there," Isidor said, supporting his sister.

"Rather him than me," Potter said. "Now put him in the boot."

"No," I told him, opening the rear passenger door. "It's inhumane."

"That's the point," Potter forced a smile at me. "He's not human."

"Neither are you," Kayla reminded him, helping Isidor place Sam on the backseat of the car.

Muttering to himself, Potter said, "Why doesn't anybody ever listen to me?" Once he had stopped moaning, he lit a cigarette and climbed in behind the wheel.

Sam lolled across the backseat, Isidor and Kayla on either side of him. Kayla gently positioned herself so Sam's head rested against her shoulder. I sat in the front passenger seat and closed the door. Potter started the car, and I looked back at the manor house, huge, dark and empty against the night sky. I wondered when we would see it again. It was the only permanent thing in our lives now. It had become our home.

I faced forward and said, "Okay, let's get going."

"You're sure about this?" Potter asked me, a smoke propped between his lips.

"Just drive," I whispered and wound down my window an inch.

Without saying another word, Potter drove us down the winding gravel path that led to the gatehouse. The car rattled over the drawbridge and I glanced at the gatehouse. I remembered being in there with Potter, where we had shared our first kiss. That seemed a lifetime ago and it had been. I was living a new life now – if I was really living at all. Once we had cleared the drawbridge, Potter stopped the car, climbed out, and closed the giant black iron gates. The wind pulled at them as if they were two giant sails. They clanked shut and Potter returned to the car, just as the first few spots of rain spattered against the windscreen.

We drove in silence, all of us, I guess, wondering what lay ahead at the Fountain of Souls. Was it like it had been the last time we had been there? As I sat nestled in my seat watching the rain lash against the windscreen, I thought of my life – the old one – it had changed in those caves beneath the fountain. That's where Murphy had died, where I had become addicted to the red stuff, and it was the place I realised I was in love with Potter. I glanced sideways, and his face was fixed with a grim look as he stared through the rain that raced down the windscreen. I knew what he was thinking – he was thinking I was wrong about going to the fountain again, but something told me that answers hid there. Another piece of the jigsaw, perhaps? I didn't have a heart to guide me anymore, but I did have a gut and it was telling me to go there. And did we have a choice? Sam was sick and needed help – where else could we take him? I couldn't just leave him to die. Besides, I needed to keep moving and not look back, because when I did, all I could see was Jack Seth's eyes burning back at me. I didn't want to think of what depraved acts he might have performed on me before finally taking my life in The Hollows. But perhaps Potter was right – maybe Jack Seth was full of shit and was just trying to unnerve me. But how could Potter be so sure?

Then, Potter spoke and dragged me from my thoughts. "We've got company," he said through gritted teeth.

"What do you mean?" I asked, glancing at him as he stared into the rear-view mirror.

"There's a cop car behind us," he said.

I glanced back over my shoulder and over the heads of Isidor, Kayla, and Sam to see the dazzling headlights of a police car tailing us in the pouring rain. "Just take it nice and easy," I told him. Remembering the nights I had often spent patrolling in the pouring rain back in Havensfield, I added, "They won't want to get out of their car on a night like this. Not if they don't have to."

Potter eased off the accelerator just a little and steadied the car as we made our way up the winding hillside. The wind blew across the open fields and valleys and buffeted the car. Thunder continued to rumble in the distance and the night sky suddenly flashed with a streak of purple lightning overhead. Rain drummed off the roof of the car and the windscreen wipers squeaked back and forth.

The police car gained on us and at first I thought it was going to overtake, but the road was too narrow and made navigating all of the tight bends too dangerous in such treacherous weather. The cop car slowed, but it was still so close that when I glanced back again, I could see the silhouette of the two giant cops wedged into the front of the car. Their size told me that perhaps they were Skin-walkers.

"Keep nice and cool, everyone," Potter whispered, glancing up into the rear-view mirror again. "Nobody do anything that might draw attention to us."

"They're just out on patrol," I said, trying to convince myself more than him.

Ahead, Potter spotted a disused garage set back from the road. Slowing the car, he steered it off the road and onto the garage forecourt.

From the darkness, we watched the police car sail past up the road.

"See, just out on patrol," I whispered.

"All the same, we'll give them a minute or two, to get way ahead of us," Potter said and lit a cigarette.

I opened the window just an inch to let out the smoke which Potter jetted from his nostrils. Kayla coughed in the background and Potter ignored her, sucking on the end of his cigarette again. Once he was done and satisfied that the cops had got some way ahead of us, Potter crushed out the cigarette end in the ashtray built into the dashboard.

"Let's go," he said, starting the car and heading back towards the road.

Lightning cracked behind the clouds overhead, and I couldn't remember a storm so bad. Rain beat down so hard against the windscreen it was almost impossible to see the road and the treacherous bends ahead.

We hadn't gone very far, when Potter glanced in the rear-view mirror and said, "I don't believe it."

"Believe what?" I said snapping my head round. Out of the back window, I could see the cop car tailing us again.

"Maybe it's a different..." I started.

"Bullshit," Potter snapped. "They're the same cops."

The Police car sped up so its front bumper was almost touching the boot of our car. Potter kept a steady speed, one eye on the road ahead, the other checking the wing mirror. The police car eased back, and Potter kept our car at the same speed.

Ahead the road widened, just a little, and the police car accelerated fast enough to pull alongside us.

We all looked right. The cop car pulled level as we stared in, the cops turned their heads to look at us. Their heads were huge and sat on broad shoulders. They were so big; it looked as if the two cops had been shoehorned into the car. Their faces were white and ill looking. Their eye sockets were sunken so far back into their faces that they looked as if the holes bored right back into their brains. Then, from deep within those holes, bright yellow light began to shine. It was like their brains had just exploded.

The cop sitting in the passenger seat lowered his window and signalled for Potter to pull over.

Potter wound down his window, the rain lashing in. "Good evening officer," he smiled. "Is there a problem?"

"Pull over!" the cop ordered, his voice a deep growl.

Knowing that we were in trouble and there was little we could do about it, Potter did what he seemed to do best and that was to inflame the situation.

"What big bright eyes, you have officer," Potter smiled. "Are they contacts or what? And the fingernails! Wow! And the strange looking faces. I love the whole Lady Gaga thing you and your friend have got going on."

26

"*Pull over!*" The skin-walker roared, its eyes flashing.

Potter wound up his window, and sped up, pulling away from the cop car.

"Why are the following us?" Kayla asked.

"Maybe they can smell your friend," Potter hissed.

No sooner had those words escaped from his mouth, then Sam began to freak out in the back of the car.

Chapter Six

Isidor

I'd just placed my free hand inside my coat, just to make sure my crossbow was within easy reach, when Sam threw his claws to his face and began to howl.

"Oh sweet-Jesus, help me!" he roared. *"I'm burning up!"* His back arched off the seat and he jerked violently forward, almost knocking Potter from his seat. The car lurched, and then stalled as the back of it skidded across the wet surface of the country road. Almost at once the night lit up in luminous flashes of blue. At first I thought it was lightning, but soon realised it wasn't, when I heard the unmistakable *whoop-whoop* sound of sirens behind us.

"I told you this was a stupid fucking idea!" Potter growled. "But, oh no – nobody ever listens to me," and I caught him shoot a glance in Kiera's direction.

Ignoring him, Kiera unfastened her seatbelt and looked back at me and Kayla. "Take hold of Sam," she hissed.

Kayla and I leant forward and wrapped our arms around Sam's naked shoulders. "He's so hot!" Kayla cried.

"For crying out loud, Kayla, now's not the time to start coming onto wolf-boy..." Potter started.

"I didn't mean it like that!" she squealed at him. "I meant he's burning up real bad back here. We need to get him some help – and fast!"

"Remember there's a couple of cops behind us," Potter shot back, as he navigated a tight bend in the road, "perhaps you could ask them."

"Very funny," Kiera snapped at him.

"Well, you're the brains, sweet-cheeks. What do we do now?" Potter glared.

"Stop the car!" Kiera answered.

"Stop the car?" we all cried at once as Sam started to convulse between Kayla and me.

"Keep him still!" Potter roared, speeding up.

"I said, *stop* the car!" Kiera shouted. "We'll never outrun them, not on roads like this and not in a storm. We'll tell them our friend is feeling ill and we're rushing him to see a doctor," she explained over the *whoop-whoop* sound and approaching thunder.

"A vet more like," Potter shouted. "Have you seen him back there with all the hair and stuff? He looks like Captain-fucking-Caveman!"

Sam howled and began to struggle with Kayla and me as we fought to restrain him. "Captain Caveman?" I asked aloud.

"Don't you *dare!*" Potter roared back at me, struggling to keep control of the speeding car. "I'm not in the mood!"

"He's the guy with the big red, white, and blue shield..." I started.

"Right, that's it! I can't bear it any longer!" Potter barked and slammed his foot down onto the brake.

There was a hissing sound as the wheels skidded to a stop on the wet road. We all flew forward in our seats, and Sam released a deafening howl. The car had only just stopped spinning when there was a bone-shaking crunch as the police car that was pursuing us smashed into the side of the car. We tail-spun out of control, and I gripped Potter's headrest with my free hand to steady myself. The world seemed to tumble out of control and it was only when my head smashed into the roof of the car that I realised we had lifted off the road and were cartwheeling through the air. Glass sprayed into the car, and I lowered my head to stop it from cutting my face and gouging my eyes out. Over the sound of crumpling metal and the thunder, I heard both Kiera and Kayla scream. Then, the world fell silent.

I opened my eyes to find myself hanging half in and half out of the back window of the car. My back was propped across the boot and my head hung down covering the number plate. I could smell petrol and it was so strong, it was suffocating. My sense of smell was greater than most, and it was at times like this I wished I couldn't smell at all. There was a squawking sound, and at first I couldn't figure out what it was. Looking at the world from upside down, I could see the police car lying on its roof, or was it the right way up? I felt so disorientated that I couldn't be sure. But the noise was coming from the broken sirens that hung from wires attached to the police car. Rain bounced up off the road and splashed my upturned face. It felt ice cold, like I was being repeatedly slapped. Stirring me from my stupor, the rain ran into my hair, and I shook my head to one side to stop it from dripping into my eyes. Then, a sudden thought took hold of me. Where were the others and were they okay?

"Kayla?" I called out, and it sounded more like a groan. Sliding from the boot of the car, I rolled into the road to find myself kneeling in muddy puddles. On my hands and knees, I scrambled alongside the overturned car and peered into the windows. Overhead, the sound of thunder boomed, and the whole world felt as if it were being rocked – *pushed*. There was a hideous cracking sound, which was closely followed by a flash of lightning that streaked across the sky. It was so bright, that just for a fraction of a second, the night turned into day. Then it was dark again, and I was struggling to see into the beat-up car. With my eyes screwed up tight, I wiped the rain from my face and could see Kayla lying face-down in the foot well between the front and back seats. Sam lay horizontally between the two front seats, looking as if he was impaled on the gearstick. On my hands and knees, I worked my way forwards and could see Kiera pressed against the cracked windscreen. Her face was turned towards me, but her eyes were closed. She looked as if she were asleep – she looked beautiful. But where was Potter? I couldn't see him.

Then there was another tearing sound, and at first, I thought it was lightning again, but there was no flash this time. I looked up to see Potter hovering above the car, his wings spread wide. They flapped in the roaring wind, sounding like sheets being buffeted about on a washing line. With one claw, he cut open the car as if he were slicing through a sheet of paper. Sparks flew up into the air as he worked quickly to remove the side of it.

"Look what you did," I shouted over the sound of the storm that was now turning wilder and fiercer with each passing second.

Raising his claws in the air, Potter said, "Cut through most things these will."

"I'm not talking about your claws!" I yelled at him. "I'm talking about what you did to us. You crashed the car. You could've killed us!"

"We're dead already," he shot back at me. "What was it the Elders called us? Dead Angels?"

"Why do you always have to be such an arrogant..." I started.

"And why do you have to be so dumb...?"

"I'm not dumb," I shouted back at him.

"So it's all an act then?" Potter yelled down at me, as he tossed the sheet of metal that he held in his hands into a nearby field.

But before I could say anything, I could see Kayla stirring in the foot well of the car. Leaping forward, I took her up in my arms and carried her to the side of the road. "Kayla?" I said, standing under the branches of a nearby tree that stretched out over the road.

"Sam?" she whispered, her eyes flickering open.

"It's me, Isidor," I told her.

"Where's Sam?" she asked, and I felt a knot of pain in my stomach as Kayla seemed more concerned for Sam than me. I was her brother. Telling myself not to be so dumb, as she could see that I was okay, I set her down on her feet and went back to the car for Sam.

Potter swooped down, plucked Kiera up into his arms, and carried her to where I had left Kayla. Leaning into the hole that Potter had ripped down the side of the car, I gripped hold of Sam's shoulders. His skin still felt hot, and he made a whimpering sound in the back of his throat like a dog that had been beat by its master.

"You're gonna be okay," I told him, as I pulled him from the car. Jeez, he was heavy. Throwing him over my shoulder, I made my way across the rain-swept road. Then, as I was heading for the trees where Kayla swayed on her feet and Potter was shaking Kiera awake, I felt Sam lift his head from my shoulder and sniff the air. He made another whimpering sound, which without warning, turned into a ferocious growl.

"Isidor, watch your back!" someone shouted as I was knocked to the ground.

Chapter Seven

Kiera

My head felt sore, and I felt something warm drip from my nose and spatter against my top lip. Somebody was holding me up and gently shaking me. I opened my eyes to see Potter staring at me.

"Kiera, are you okay?" he was asking me, but his voice was groggy, as if coming from far away. I felt my legs begin to buckle at the knees and he gripped me by the shoulders. "Kiera?" he said again.

Then I remembered him shouting at Isidor and breaking hard. I could see the world tumbling out of control and my face hitting the windshield.

"You arsehole," I mumbled and went to slap his face. But I was still disorientated and he easily took hold of my wrist.

"Don't get so excited, sweet-cheeks," he half-smiled at me.

"You crashed the car on purpose," I said, my eyesight starting to focus again, and the feeling returning to my legs.

"It worked though, didn't it? Those cops are dead," he said, looking back over his shoulder at the police car, which now sat on its roof spraying flashes of blue light into the night from its crushed emergency lights. Then, letting go of me, Potter shouted, *"Isidor watch your back!"*

As if the world had been paused, I watched as two guys in police uniforms sprang from beneath the upturned car and into the air. Their transformation from man to wolf was so rapid that if I'd blinked, I would have missed it. Their crisp, white shirts, their trousers, and their boots flew away in ragged strips, revealing the giant wolves that hid beneath them. With snouts similar in size to that of a lion's, the two wolves launched themselves at Isidor. Everything happened so fast, that Isidor was unaware of the creatures that were about to rip him to pieces, just like their clothes that now fluttered away in the raging wind.

"Isidor!" Kayla shrieked, and I snapped my head right, to see her standing next to me in the pouring rain.

There was a vicious-sounding snarl that was so loud that I threw my hands to my ears. I watched Isidor glance up at Potter as he raced towards him. And as fast as the wolves had shed their uniforms, Potter had removed his long, black coat, his wings were out, and he was speeding through the air. Realising that something wasn't right, Isidor spun around. It was then that I saw the wolf on his back. It was Sam. The boy's face was still half human and half wolf and his eyes glowed so bright that they looked like headlamps. He opened his mouth, foamy lengths of saliva swinging from his ivory-looking teeth. Sam threw his head back and roared. Fearing that he was going to tear Isidor's head from his neck, my claws and fangs sprung out without me having to think about it. It was as natural as breathing to me now. With my head still feeling foggy, I was just about to spring into the air, when I was grabbed from behind. Swiping my claws in the air, I spun around as Kayla ducked to avoid me taking her head clean off. It was Kayla who had hold of me.

"Let go of me!" I shouted at her.

"Look!" she cried, pointing back at Isidor.

I glanced back over my shoulder to see Sam leap from Isidor's back and drag one of the Skin-walkers out of the air.

"Sam's helping Isidor," Kayla shouted over a sudden rumble of thunder. "Sam won't hurt him."

Isidor fell forward onto his knees, rolled over, and within an instant he was on his feet again, crossbow in hand and firing off wave after wave of stakes at the Skin-walkers. Potter snatched the second Skin-walker from the air by wrapping his arms around the creature and dragging him away from Isidor. He flew backwards into the air. The wolf kicked wildly with its huge back legs. With the creature's chest exposed, Isidor seized his chance and filled it with stakes that whizzed through the air with lightning speed.

With the wolf going limp in Potter's arms, he threw it aside and performed something close to a loop-de-loop in the air above the road. I felt Kayla loosen her grip on me. She was then flashing past as she raced across the road towards Sam, who was now lying on his back and struggling to fight off the Skin-walker that was poised over him. Just like the rest of us, Kayla released her fangs and claws, throwing off her coat so her glitter-coated wings could be freed.

Screeching like a wild bird of prey, she shot through the dark and clattered into the wolf that was now biting and snapping at Sam. The wolf looked confused, though, like he wasn't sure whether to kill one of his own. Maybe he couldn't figure out what the odd-looking wolf-boy was. But in those few seconds of doubt, Kayla sunk her fangs into its neck. Blood jetted from its throat and turned her face the same colour as her hair. I could see her throat bobbing up and down as she drank from the wolf. Her eyes rolled back in their sockets, showing their whites. She looked as if she were in ecstasy.

The Skin-walker went crazy as it lashed out with his giant paws and snapped at the air with its teeth. It howled and roared, black jets of blood shooting from its mouth like vomit.

"Kayla!" I roared, pulling her from the wolf, fearing that if she drank too much of the red stuff, her cravings would never again be sedated by Lot 13.

She made a gargling sound in the back of her throat as she momentarily tried to fight me off. I gripped hold of her and watched as the wolf's blood ran from the corners of her mouth. My stomach began to cramp as I fought my own sudden urge to let go of her and drink from the wolf myself. Watching the thick, black globules of blood drip from her chin made my head spin, and I looked down at my claws which held her, and saw that the skin on them was starting to crack. I released her, and she fell backwards onto her arse and into the nearest puddle. With my claws held out before me, I gasped in horror as my flesh turned grey and began to break. My claws disappeared back into my fingertips and the cracks went with them. But those sick, cramping feelings in my stomach remained, and the urge for the red stuff was stronger than ever before.

Wheeling around, I watched as the wolf that Kayla had fed on struggled to its feet. It whimpered and then collapsed onto its side as Potter dropped from the sky and removed its head with one quick swipe of his claws. Blood pumped from its neck and clouded the puddles that covered the road. With my eyes fixed on the blood, I stepped forward, as if I were sleepwalking. I ran the tip of my tongue over my lips. All I could see was the blood. The wind and the driving rain had gone, everything had gone, except the red stuff pumping from the neck of the Skin-walker.

"No," someone whispered in my ear.

As if waking from a dream, I looked right and could see Potter.

"No, Kiera," he said again, and took my hand. "You don't need that."

"But..." I started.

"Later," he said back.

"I'm cracking up in more ways than one," I told him, feeling scared all of a sudden.

"I'll take care of you," he said, gently squeezing my hand.

"Someone give me a hand over here!" Isidor shouted, as the sky lit up with another fork of lightning.

Potter let go of my hand and ran through the rain towards Isidor, who was trying to lift Sam off the road. I looked down one last time at the blood leaking from the wolf, and reluctantly crossed the road to join them.

"We need to get him some help - and quick," Isidor said, crouching, so he could place one of Sam's arms around his shoulders. Sam's black hair, which covered his cheeks and chin, glistened with rain and was matted and tangled.

"We should leave him," Potter said. "He's not one of us."

"He saved Isidor," Kayla spoke up from behind us. We turned around to see her get up from the puddles, arming the blood away from her mouth.

"We can't trust him," Potter snapped.

"He attacked one of his own to protect Isidor," she came back at him, wiping the water from the seat of her jeans.

"So you admit that he is one of them?" Potter shot back.

"Look, until we know for sure what he is, Sam comes with us," I cut in. "We can't just leave him. He is obviously going through some kinda change. And Kayla's right. He did help Isidor."

"I think he's part wolf and part human," Isidor said.

"No shit, Sherlock!" Potter glared, picking his coat up off the road and putting it on.

"Why do you have to always..." Isidor started, but Potter spoke over him.

"Look, it isn't going to take the Skin-walkers long to figure out what just happened here, and they'll come after us," he said. "We need to get away from here fast. The wolf-boy will only slow us down."

"We could fly," Kayla suggested, helping Isidor get Sam to his feet.

"What, in this storm?" Potter asked, glancing up at the night sky as it split in two with more flashes of purple lightning. "It's too dangerous. And besides, I don't fancy being the one carrying wolf-boy when he decides to start fitting again."

"We go on foot then," I said. "We find some shelter until the storm passes, and by then, Sam's fever might have passed."

"Whatever we're gonna do, we better decide quickly," Isidor said and pointed into the distance. "It looks like we've got company sooner than we thought."

I looked in the direction he was pointing and across the bleak fields, I could see flashes of blue and white light. At first I thought that Isidor was wrong and the blue shocks of light were the storm. But the flashes of blue were coming closer and at speed. It was the emergency lights of police cars that I could see.

"Potter, help me get our stuff from the boot," I snapped, racing towards the car. I knocked my wet hair from my eyes and fumbled with the lock on the car, but it was jammed, busted shut during the crash.

Potter pushed me aside as the sound of police sirens grew ever louder behind us. Making a fist with his claw, he smashed through the boot, peeling back the metal, like opening up a can of beans. Reaching into the hole that he had made, Potter yanked out our backpacks.

"Take these," he said, piling the bags into my arms. "Now get the others into that field and run."

"What about you?" I asked.

Potter took his lighter from his pocket and said, "I'm gonna get rid of any trace that we've been here." Then turning, he stuck his lighter to the petrol that bled from the car. The petrol lit at once, and a streak of blue and orange flame raced towards the car. "Run!" he roared, as we were lifted off our feet and thrown into the air under the force of the explosion.

Chapter Eight

Kiera

I landed on my arse with a thump. Potter hit the ground just feet from me. The rucksacks I'd been holding were next to me. The sky looked like it was on fire, as a huge cloud of smoke and flame belched up into the night. Even though I was now twenty feet away or more in a nearby field, I could feel the heat of the burning car against my skin.

Isidor and Kayla stumbled towards us, Sam hanging limp between them. The sound of approaching police cars was almost deafening, barely drowned out by the booming thunder and crackles of lightning above us. I scrambled to my feet, my clothes, hands, and face spattered with mud. The ground was boggy, and was like walking in quicksand, making each step that I took sluggish, as if I were drunk. Potter sat in the field, and I glanced back to see him pop a cigarette between his lips and light it. He looked as if he were relaxing at some picnic.

I reached Isidor and Kayla as they struggled across the field with Sam. "Here, let me help you," I said, taking hold of him.

"Help me get him onto my shoulder," Isidor asked.

Together, Kayla and I hoisted Sam over Isidor's shoulder. Sam's arms were so long, that they hung down the length of Isidor's back, almost brushing against the muddy field. I looked at Isidor as he lumbered forward, his ear piercing twinkling in the night. His black hair hung over his eyes, and the tattoos that covered his neck were lost to the shadows. For the first time, Isidor looked older than eighteen. That boyish look was fading from his face, and I could see that he was turning into a man. But Isidor didn't look happy. I don't mean that any of us were overjoyed about the new world that we found ourselves in, but he looked troubled, as if he had something on his mind that he couldn't bring himself to talk about. I wanted to chat with him, ask what was wrong, but now wasn't the time – but when was the best time?

From the other side of the stone wall that circled the field I could hear the sound of the police cars screaming to a halt. Doors swung open and then were slammed shut. The faint sound of garbled radio messages hissed over the noise of the rolling thunder.

"They're going to start searching the area," Kayla whispered, her eyes wide with fright.

"How do you know?" I whispered back.

"Heard one of those cops talking into his radio," she said. "They were asking for Berserkers to be brought in to help track us."

"Berserkers?" I breathed, knowing that I'd heard that name before.

"Remember, I found out about them on the Internet," Isidor reminded me. "They're the wolves that don't match properly with humans. They go so crazy that they either get shot or locked up. They're vicious killers."

I glanced at Sam as he dangled over Isidor's shoulder. *Wolves that didn't match well with their human host*, I thought to myself, then pushed the thought from my mind. Then, spying Potter still sitting on his arse and enjoying his cigarette, I shouted, "Are you coming, or what?"

"Where?" he said. "You know, I've been thinking, perhaps we should stay and fight, instead of all this sneaking about?"

"They're sending Berserkers after us," I snapped, as I threw one of the rucksacks over my shoulder and the other two at him. "You stay and fight if you want to."

I'd never seen Potter look scared of anything before, but hearing me mention the word *Berserkers*, he flicked his cigarette away, snatched up the rucksacks and jumped to his feet. "This way," he ordered, and started off across the field.

We had walked for half an hour perhaps, when we found ourselves in a deep valley. The field had given way to a narrow path that weaved its way between two hills. The ground had become rocky, and slabs of black granite jutted through the earth. The wind still roared around us, and every so often, loose lumps of rock would break free in the wind and clatter down the hillside towards us. The sky was covered in a thick layer of cloud, which looked knotted and swollen. Lightning flashed deep within it, turning the night sky mauve then blue. Before entering the valley, I glanced back one last time in the direction that we had come from and could just make out the orange glow and a spiral of smoke coming from the car that Potter had torched. I faced front again, Potter striding ahead out front, Kayla and Isidor walking silently together as Sam hung over Isidor's shoulder.

Berserkers I feared, and hurried after the others.

We walked in silence, all of us. It was miserable. The storm blew so hard now, that for most of the journey, we walked, hunched forward, our bodies battered by the wind and driving rain. Isidor stumbled on, and twice Potter went to him and asked to take Sam. But twice, Isidor just silently shook his head and trudged forward. It was like Isidor had something to prove, but was it to us or himself, I wondered.

After two hours or more of walking, the valley opened out in to a wide, flat area. It was barren and bleak-looking. The ground was flat and covered in wild grass, which looked almost silver in the dark. Ancient trees stood at irregular intervals, and looked twisted and bent out of shape. The knotted branches were leafless, and stooped over like the elderly. Wales could be cold at the best of times, but this was ridiculous. I couldn't ever remember feeling so wet through and cold. I just wanted to lie down. The Fountain of Souls was hundreds of miles away, and I had no idea of how we would get there. We needed rest more than anything, and a chance to think of a plan.

Then, when I was on the verge of giving up and contemplating Potter's idea of standing and fighting instead of going on the run, he called out to me.

"Hey, take a look at this," he said, waving us towards him with his hand.

We made our way over the uneven ground and joined him. Through the overgrown grass, I could just make out a set of railway tracks. It looked rusty and worn; the wooden sleepers fixed between them were covered in moss. It looked as if a train hadn't passed through here in years.

"So?" Kayla asked sullenly, and I could sense that the storm and the cold had gotten to her, too.

"I know it doesn't look as if it's been used in ages," Potter started to explain, "but it could lead us to a set of tracks that are in use. There might be goods trains. We could maybe hide on board and get out of here. We could be miles away in just hours."

"We could get some rest," I said hopefully.

"And get out of this rain," Kayla muttered.

"Let's just get going," Isidor spoke up, repositioning Sam onto his other shoulder. The boy looked asleep, as Isidor supported him across his back.

"What have we got to lose?" Potter shrugged, and set off along the tracks.

In single file we followed him, walking between the running rails. The tracks weaved across the desolate moorland, without a sign of any trains, or even life for that matter. It felt as if we were the only creatures alive. But I knew that was not true. There would be a whole army of Skin-walkers searching for us already. We had walked for another hour or two, and I wondered how late it was. It must have been at least two in the morning by now. Then, in the distance, I could see a small squat-shaped building. I peered through the darkness at it, but couldn't tell if it was a house or some other type of building. I pointed out the structure to Potter and with caution, we made our way towards it.

As we grew closer, I could see that it was a small railway station and the tracks were winding towards it. About a quarter of a mile from the station, we reached a set of points in the track. They were overgrown with weeds and wildflowers. But Potter had been right; there was a set of gleaming silver tracks leading from the points. By the look of it, the other set of tracks appeared to be regularly used by passing trains.

As if knowing what I was thinking, Potter winked at me and said, "See, tiger, I was right." Then, he was gone, heading down the tracks towards the station.

There was a single platform, and we climbed up onto it. Reaching up, Isidor passed Sam into Kayla's arms so he could climb onto the platform. I could see two wooden benches and a wooden door which led into what looked like a small waiting room. At one end of the platform there was a sign erected to a tall wooden post. The sign swung back and forth in the wind on a pair of rusty hinges. *The Great Western Railway,* the sign read.

The station was constructed of grey brick and a wooden canopy hung overhead, which offered some protection from the bitterly cold wind and rain. Potter pushed against the waiting room door, it swung open and we followed him inside. I'd never seen such an ancient-looking waiting room in my life. It looked like it hadn't been modernised since The Second World War. Set in the wall by the door was a tiny kiosk which had been constructed from wood. Behind this, there was a chair and decrepit-looking ticket machine and cash register. The ticket office was still in use, as it was free from dust, and several pencils had been neatly lined in a row on the other side of the counter by whoever worked here.

The floor of the waiting room was made of stone, and had been swept clean. Beside the ticket office were several wooden levers, which I guessed worked the points that we had come across further down the tracks. These huge levers did look unused, and above them, written on a dog-eared piece of paper, were two words that had long since faded in the sunlight, which must have streamed through the windows during the summer months. But even though the two words were just a washed out grey, I could just about read them. Written above one set of levers was the word *PULL.* Above the other set, *PUSH.*

I turned away and could see three long benches set against the walls of the waiting room; but unlike the seats on the platform, these were cushioned in green leather. There was another door, and I watched Potter open it and disappear. Isidor and Kayla laid Sam on one of the seats. Kayla sat beside him. She looked down and gently brushed the fur that covered his cheeks.

"How's he doing?" I asked her.

"I think the fever might be easing a bit," she said, her eyes full of hope.

"You like him, don't you?" I asked, going over to her.

"He's my friend," she smiled, not taking her eyes off him. "We stuck together at Ravenwood School. "Sam's only like this because he tried to help me."

"Let's hope that fever breaks then," I said thoughtfully. "But just be careful, okay?"

"Careful of what?" she asked, and this time she did look at me.

Thinking of the Berserkers, but not wanting to scare her, I said, "Just be careful. We don't know what's wrong with Sam."

Not wanting to get into a debate with her, I was glad when Potter stepped back into the waiting room and said, "There's a small kitchen back here. There isn't much, but there's some bread and a pot of coffee that we could heat up."

"It's not coffee I want," Kayla said, glancing at the bag I was carrying.

"Suit yourselves," Potter shrugged, crossing the waiting room and going to the door. "Before we settle down, I'm going to make sure that there's no one else around." Then, he was gone, stepping back out onto the platform and into the storm.

Without saying a word, I handed my rucksack to Kayla. Unhesitatingly, she unfastened it and removed three tubes of Lot 13. Kayla handed one to Isidor and offered me the other.

"No thanks," I said.

"Okay," Kayla sighed. She unscrewed the remaining bottle, tilted back her head, and poured the thick pink liquid into her mouth.

With my stomach beginning to cramp for the red stuff, I went after Potter. The platform was deserted. I made my way along it, when suddenly I was grabbed and dragged through a door set into the wall halfway up the platform. I found myself in a bathroom. There was no lighting, but I could see him clearly enough in the dark. Potter locked the door behind me, and as if knowing why I had gone in search of him, he rolled down the collar of his coat and turned his neck towards me. Without saying anything, I darted across the bathroom and sank my teeth into his neck. Blood washed into my mouth, and it tasted coppery and sweet. It felt hot as it gushed over my tongue and down my throat. As his blood hit the pit of my stomach, the cramps eased. Even so, I kept drinking from him. Potter held me in his arms, and I felt him shudder against me.

Slowly, he eased me off him but I didn't want to stop, not just yet, and I tried to bite his neck again. The cramps inside me became nothing more than a series of butterflies, and I knew that it was more than just his blood that I now wanted. Potter entwined his fingers in my hair and pulled my face towards his. I only had to look into his black eyes to see that by sharing his blood with me, he now wanted his fill. Roughly, he pressed his lips against my mouth, and I could feel his tongue wrap itself around mine. With his free hand, he started to pull my coat from me. I felt it slide down my back and onto the floor. He then ran his fingers up the length of my neck. Finding a vein pulsating just beneath the surface of my skin, he plunged his fangs into it. At once I felt dizzy and lightheaded as my blood pumped into his mouth. How long he drank from me, I do not know; but when I felt so dizzy that I was sure I was going to faint, Potter took his mouth from my neck.

Then, kissing my mouth again, he pushed me against the sink where he put his hand up my top and ran them across my breasts. With my head spinning and feeling dizzy, I loosened the buckle that held up his trousers and worked them down. Removing his hands from beneath my top, he hurriedly yanked my jeans down over my hips and turned me away from him.

"You want this, don't you?" He breathed down my neck.

"You know I need you," I pleaded. Pressing the flats of my hands against the mirror, Potter pushed himself into me.

Our lovemaking was quick, almost frenzied, the act of drinking one another's blood turning us both on. I didn't understand why or how, but just like in the summerhouse, it was an act so intense and intimate, that it made my whole body ache for him. The climax of our lovemaking was like a wave of unbearable pleasure. Turning me around to face him again, Potter pressed his lips over mine, and I felt his rough stubble prickle my skin like needlepoints. Our kissing was as passionate as was our lovemaking again, and still I felt unsatisfied. With a shove of my claws, I pushed him away from me. He crashed into the wall, shattering the mirror fixed to it.

Taking hold of him, I pushed him down onto the floor. Kicking my jeans free, I lowered myself onto him and as I did, I covered his chest with kisses. His skin felt cold and tight, his chest firm. Moving my hips back and forth on him, he closed his eyes, as my hair dangled just inches from his face. Losing his fingers in it, he pulled my face towards his, but instead of kissing my lips, he covered my breasts with his mouth. He freed one of his hands from my hair and traced his claws down the small of my back. His touch was light, but painful, and I arched my back and shuddered. Then, forcing me onto my back and pinning my wrists to the floor, Potter made love to me again. But this time, it was slower, each movement more deliberate and precise than the last. I wrapped my legs around his back and pulled him deeper into me. At that moment, nothing else seemed to matter; it was like nothing else existed apart from me and Potter.

"I love you, tiger," he panted, his voice sounding broken.

"I love you more," I breathed, when all I wanted to do was scream it out loud.

"Sometimes making love to you isn't enough," he gasped. "I want more of you. You drive me fucking insane."

"And drinking my blood – isn't that enough?" I moaned, as he moved faster above me.

"It's a start," he whispered and continued to make love to me until we both collapsed in each other's arms.

When we returned to the waiting room sometime later, Sam was still asleep on one of the leather benches, and Kayla was curled up on the other. She opened her eyes as we came in, the wind blowing in behind us.

"Did you see anyone?" she asked.

"No", Potter said, before I'd the chance to say anything.

Isidor was looking at the levers sticking out from the wall to the left of the tiny ticket office. Hearing us come in, he looked around and said, "Look what I found."

He held up an old-fashioned radio.

"Great, we'll be able to have a party," Potter said, hunkering down on the floor, where he made himself comfortable by leaning against the wall and crossing his feet at the ankles.

"Actually, I can't get a signal," Isidor told him. "All I can get is static. We must be too remote."

I cuddled up next to Potter and glanced at Sam. His skin didn't look so sallow as before and his face was no longer covered in sweat. *Perhaps his fever had broken after all,* I thought.

"So what do we do now?" Isidor asked, sitting on the last remaining bench.

"We wait for the storm to clear," I said. "Hopefully it will have eased by morning." Then, as if speaking too soon, the night sky fizzled with lightning and a clash of thunder. Rain battered the windows, and I could hear it drumming off the waiting room roof.

"And what if a train doesn't come through?" Isidor asked. "This place doesn't look as if it's like a main commuter station or anything like that."

"Then we think of something else," Potter said, half closing his eyes. "You know, we use our brains. I know that puts you at an unfair disadvantage, Isidor."

"Fuck off!" Isidor suddenly said.

I was shocked to hear him say this, as I couldn't ever recall hearing Isidor swear. Potter looked just as shocked, as he opened his eyes and stared at Isidor. With half a smile tugging at the corner of his lips, Potter said, "What did you say?"

"I told you to fuck off," Isidor snapped again, and I could hear anger – frustration – bubbling away in his voice. "What, has your ego got so fucking big that it's covered your ears and made you deaf?"

"Isidor," Kayla gasped and sat up. "What's gotten into you?"

"He has," Isidor barked and pointed at Potter. "I'm sick and tired of him taking the piss out of me all the time."

"Look, can we do this tomorrow or something?" Potter moaned. "I need some sleep. We all do, by the look of things."

"The only thing I'm tired of around here, is you," Isidor spat, staring at Potter.

"Okay, kid..." Potter started.

"And I'm not a fucking kid!" Isidor shouted. "I'm eighteen years old. Stop treating me like a child."

"Grow up then," Potter shouted back. "You're always coming out with dumb stuff all the time."

"Okay, so I don't know as much as you do about cartoons and stuff," Isidor snapped back at him. "But who really gives a shit about Scooby-Doo, Captain-fucking-Caveman, or some stupid mouse?"

"Stuart Little," Potter smiled.

"Who gives a shit!" Isidor almost screamed and stood up. "You don't know anything about me. You only know what I've told you."

"So why haven't you told us?" I asked softly, seeing that Isidor was really upset.

"Because people never listen to me!" he roared. "Everyone just thinks I'm dumb. Good old Isidor. He's good to have around in a fight – but I'm not much more than that. But I am more. I know I'm more."

"Like what?" I asked him, my voice still soft and compassionate.

"Like I knew that Luke was really Elias Munn," he said. "I knew it was him back in The Hollows, but I was too scared to say anything."

"Why?" I asked him.

"Would you have believed me?" Isidor shouted. "No – you would've just taken the piss. Potter would have taken the piss. He would've called me numb nuts." Then, turning on Potter, Isidor said, "You wouldn't have believed me because Luke was your friend – he was your best mate – and I wasn't. I was just the joker in the pack – Shaggy-fucking-Doo. Just like Shaggy-Doo, I provide the laughs. He never gets to solve the mystery, does he? It's always the others – the clever ones. Well, I did solve the mystery way before any of you, but I sat back and let that animal kill my sister, then murder me, because I was just too fucking scared to speak up."

"Scared of what?" I asked, starting to feel ashamed of myself for not knowing that he had been feeling like this for so long.

"I was scared that you wouldn't believe me – that you would call me stupid," and he looked at Potter, who sat on the floor, that look of arrogance wiped from his face. "But I do know stuff and I can't stay silent again. I don't care if you laugh and take the piss out of me. I don't care what you call me. I won't watch my friends walk into danger again."

"What do you know?" Potter asked him, and for once, Potter spoke to him as his equal.

Taking a deep breath as if trying to calm himself, Isidor finally said, "I've seen that word *push* before."

"Where?" Potter asked, his eyes narrowing.

"I saw it before the world was even *pushed*, if that makes sense," Isidor told us. "And I have the proof right here."

"What proof?" I asked him gently.

Patting his chest, Isidor said, "Right in here."

Then, sitting down again on the bench, and with the storm howling outside, Isidor began to talk. This is what he told us.

Chapter Nine

Isidor

Melody Rose stood out from the rest. Not because of anything she said or did, it was her ordinariness, that's what drew attention to her.

I was fourteen, and had never dared leave The Hollows, not once. Some of the other Vampyrus I hung out with had shared stories of how they had snuck above ground. I was fascinated by what they told me, although some of what I heard I wondered if it was even true. It wasn't as if I didn't know anything about how the humans lived and the inventions that they had created. Over hundreds of years, other Vampyrus who had ventured above ground had returned with picture books, magazines, and newspapers. One Vampyrus, he was just a kid, I think his name was Burton, had returned one day with this odd-looking contraption, which shone moving pictures against the cave walls. It was like magic. He said the humans called it a *movie projector*.

My mum, well, the woman who I believed to be my mother, told me how many years before I'd been born, Burton had returned below ground with a magical roll of pictures. Claiming that he had magic moving pictures of the most beautiful creature that had ever existed below or above ground, he gathered as many Vampyrus into the great chamber beneath the Dewy Pyramids and projected the magic pictures of this most beautiful human. As he stood before the hundreds of Vampyrus crammed into the chamber before him, Burton proudly announced that her name was Marilyn Monroe. During that short clip of film, my mother told me how the male Vampyrus had whooped, whistled, and cheered as she had stood in a flowing white dress which rippled up around her thighs. With a wistful smile on her face, my mother told me it was because of those magical moving pictures of that beautiful woman that hundreds of male Vampyrus left The Hollows the following day in search of their own creature as stunning as the one they had seen on the chamber walls.

When I asked my mother what had become of this Burton, who had loved the magic moving pictures, she explained that, like the others, he had disappeared above ground.

"Some say that he fell so in love with those moving pictures, that he spent the rest of his life learning how to make his own," she said.

I loved hearing stories about above ground and I wanted to be able to tell my own. The humans sounded magical to me. They had so much and did so much. But the one thing that grabbed my attention the most – and I just couldn't believe it to be true – was that humans wanted to be the same. They didn't like other humans who were different in any way. I got the feeling that it scared them. But I wouldn't know for sure unless I ventured above ground and saw these humans for myself.

My mother never knew of my adventures above ground – not until much later, that is. Once I'd made up my mind to go above ground, it took me about a week to pluck up the courage to venture out of The Hollows. It took me three days to find a route that I was happy with. I could have followed the paths that my friends and had taken, but I wanted my own. I didn't want mother to find out, you see. I wouldn't find out for some years why she was scared of me going above ground. Perhaps she was worried, that like the kid Burton, I would fall in love with something and never go back to her.

The path I finally chose I found by chance. I lived with my mother in a hollow carved into the face of the Ageless Hill. I often wandered alone, conjuring stories inside my head about the world I had yet to see which existed above me. It was while I was walking one chilly afternoon that I noticed a root which protruded through the ground from above. It was so cold, the root was covered in a white frost and it glistened above like a stalagmite.

I stood on tiptoe and reached up for the root. I gripped it, but the knotted lump of tree was slippery and I lost my hold and footing and landed on my arse. With the wind knocked from me, I tried again until I finally managed to work my way up it. Looking back below to make sure I wasn't being watched, I placed one cold hand over the other and disappeared in amongst the roots of the tree.

Spiderpeeds and slugworms dropped from the roots as I cut a path through them. They wriggled in my hair, and I shook the insects free by shaking my head wildly from side to side. Then when I thought I couldn't climb any further, I found a hole. Taking a deep breath, I made myself as small as possible and wriggled into it. It was dark, but the roots gave way, and I found myself crawling on my hands and knees down a tunnel made of brick. The walls and ground felt slimy, and several times I had to stop dead-still as rats scurried past me. I hate rats. I didn't know how long or how far I had crawled through the tunnel, but I got the feeling that the tunnel was climbing upwards. Then, ever so gradually, I could see my hands in front of me along with the green and yellow moss that covered the walls of the tunnel. I looked up to see light shining through a metal grate. It was the first time that I had seen sunlight. It shone through the holes in the grate in thin, white slices. In that light, I spied a ladder fixed to the wall. Looking back one last time in the direction that I had come, I mustered all my courage and climbed the ladder towards the light. I had always had a heightened sense of smell, but now my nose tingled with the new wave of scents that wafted down the tunnel. Although the scent was sweet – almost fresh – I could also detect a metallic smell in the air.

I poked my fingers through the holes in the grate and felt the wind sweep over my fingers. It felt cold, just like the air in The Hollows. Gritting my teeth together, I lifted up the grate and slid it to one side. The sunlight showered my face. I closed my eyes and let it shine upon me. I stayed like that for several minutes, my head sticking up out of the hole, while the sun and wind touched my face. It felt incredible. With my heart racing, I opened my eyes and hoisted myself out of the hole. I pushed the grate back into place, then looked about me. I found myself standing in a large wooded area. The trees were similar to those in The Hollows, and they stretched up into the sky. The sky! Oh my God – the sky. I had only ever seen it in pictures and now I was actually standing beneath it. I stared upwards through the canopy of fine green leaves and drew a breath. To get a better look, I made my way through the trees until I found myself out in the open and standing on a narrow road. The sky was a pale blue and wispy clouds covered it like big white scratches. I heard from my friends that if you stared at the clouds long enough, you would see pictures in them, like faces, monsters, and all sorts of other weird stuff.

So with my head tilted back, I stood in the road and gazed up at the sky. But before any of those faces and monsters had had a chance to appear for me, there was a bellowing sound. I span around to see a car bearing down on me. I had seen cars in picture books, but nothing could have prepared me for the speed with which they travelled. Stumbling backwards, the car raced past in a streak of silver. I could smell that metallic scent again and it came from a pipe which jutted out from the back of the car. As it passed me by, the driver jabbed his middle finger into the air and screamed, "Get out of the fucking road, arsehole!"

I wasn't too familiar with how humans greeted one another, but I got the feeling that the guy driving the car wasn't too pleased to see me. The car disappeared into the distance, and taking more care, I headed down the road in the direction that the car had gone. I'd walked for some time, stopping every now and then when something caught my eye. There seemed to be so much to take in that my mind started to race, and I couldn't wait to get back to The Hollows and tell my friends my own stories. But the thing that caught my imagination the most was the birds. We had flying creatures in The Hollows, I was one of them.

I knew from the stories I had been told, that unlike us, humans couldn't fly. They wanted to – they dreamt about it all the time. So they had invented machines called aeroplanes which they sat in and travelled through the air with. Listening to these stories, I had learnt from a very young age that any

Vampyrus venturing above ground should never reveal their wings to the humans.

"Remember, humans don't like anything that is different," my mother had often warned me, her green eyes growing wide as if she were telling me a scary bedtime story. "If they were to ever find out that winged creatures were living just beneath them, they would come in search of us."

"But why?" I would ask her.

"Because, they don't like *different*, Isidor. They like everyone to be the same," she would whisper while stoking the fire. Then, looking back over her shoulder at me with the flames dancing in her eyes, she would add, "They would capture us, put us in cages, and open us up to see how we worked."

I would often lie awake at night, my fingertips tracing the angry-looking scars that ran down the inside of my arms. Behind them hid my wings. When my wings were out, the scars disappeared, but my mother would warn me not to get them out too often as they would get stuck like that one day. And she was right, because one day, they did.

So pulling my coat about me, paranoid that some human might see my scars, I continued to follow the road. After a couple of miles or so, I came to a wooden sign that had been fixed to the trunk of a large tree.

Welcome to Lake Lure – Please drive carefully had been stencilled across it in thick, black letters. Staring at the sign, I guessed the last part had been added for the guy who had called me an arsehole.

I pulled the collar of my coat up around my neck, thrust my hands into my pockets, and headed towards the town of Lake Lure. I wondered what stories I might find there.

Chapter Ten

Isidor

I remember seeing Melody Rose as I made my way through the town of Lake Lure. The town was a crisscross of narrow streets, and each one was lined with tired-looking shops and houses. People passed along the streets and between the narrow alleyways that separated the buildings. At first I feared that everyone would stare at me, that they would know I was different to them somehow. I was paranoid that they would stop and point at me because of those scars that ran down the length of my arms. But no one paid any attention to me at all. All of them seemed too busy and preoccupied with their own lives and daily business to even look at me.

As I crossed the main street, which seemed to cut the town in two, I heard someone shout, "Leave me alone!"

The voice was female and she sounded more frustrated than scared. I stopped on the pavement and waited to see if the girl's voice came again. It did.

"Don't touch me!" and this time, the owner of the voice sounded upset.

I followed the sound into a narrow alley that ran between a restaurant and clothes shop. Down one side of the alley stood several large rubbish bins. Each of them was spilling over with rotten food, which I guessed had come from the restaurant. The stench made me want to puke, so I covered my nose with my hands. It was then, as I passed the bins, that I saw Melody for the first time. There were others gathered around her, but it was Melody I saw first.

Her hair was mousey coloured and pulled back into a bun at the nape of her neck. On her head she wore a dark bonnet which was secured beneath her chin with a length of black cord. Her skin was pale and there was no colour to her cheeks. She wore a plain grey dress with long sleeves, and the hem hung just above a pair of uncomfortable-looking boots.

Over her dress she looked to be wearing some kind of off-white coloured apron, which had a big pocket across the front, like a kangaroo pouch. From where I hid behind the rubbish bins, the girl looked to be about fourteen, the same as me.

I could see three other teenagers with her. Two of them were boys, and the other a girl. Unlike Melody, the others wore denim jeans, trainers, and T-shirts. One of the boys seemed to be keeping lookout, as he was glancing up and down the alleyway. His front teeth jutted over his bottom lip and a stream of drool swung from his chin. His hair was short and black, and had been combed into spikes on top of his head.

I watched as this boy turned to the others and said, "Hurry up!" He sounded excited and nervous all at the same time as he glanced back down the alley towards the main road.

"You don't say much," the other boy said to Melody as he stuck his hands into the pocket that covered Melody's apron.

"Leave me alone," Melody said softly, trying to pull the boy's hand from her dress.

From my hiding place crouched behind the bins, I watched as the girl, who had blonde hair, step forward and hold Melody's hands against the alley wall as the boy riffled through her pocket.

"I said, you don't say much," he said again. "Dumb, are ya?"

Melody just stared at him with a pair of pale blue eyes.

"Got nuffin' to say for yourself?" the girl smirked, and I could see she was taking pleasure at tormenting Melody.

"'Hurry up!" the boy keeping watch said again, looking back over his shoulder to make sure that they were still alone.

Then, as if finding the winning lottery ticket, the boy pulled something from the huge pocket on Melody's apron and yelped, "What do we 'ave here then?"

I peered through a gap in the bins and saw what looked like some kind of chain hanging from the boy's fist. He taunted Melody with it by swinging it back and forth in front of her face. It was long and black and seemed to be made of beads. Attached to it was a cross.

"What's this then?" the boy sneered, and for the first time, I could see that his forehead and cheeks were covered in sore-looking pimples.

"Oh, isn't it pretty!" the girl mocked, releasing Melody's hands so she could take a better look.

"It's a necklace," the kid with the buckteeth sniggered, spraying a stream of spit from his lips.

Holding it in front of Melody's face, the kid with the zits snapped, "Is it worth anything?"

Melody remained silent, never taking her eyes off her tormentors. Her face was paper white and however much she tried to hide it, I could see she was scared and I could smell her fear. I'd put up with my own fair amount of shit from bullies in the past because they thought I was thick, but I had learnt not be scared of them.

"It's one of those religious thingies!" the girl chirped up. "I think it's some sorta good luck charm or something."

"Oooh!" the boy with the spots smirked. "Magic, is it?" and he swung the rosary beads like a pendulum in front of Melody's face.

Melody just stared back at him.

"Do you want it back?" he asked.

Melody nodded.

"Go on, take them," he taunted.

I watched Melody look at the chain as it was waved before her.

"Go on, take it!" the girl urged with excitement.

Melody slowly raised her hand and reached for the chain, but spotty snatched them away. This sent the girl and the kid with the teeth rolling about in a fit of hysterics.

"You weren't quick enough, holy-girl," spotty teased. Then, bringing the chain within Melody's reach again, he said, "Go on, take it."

At first Melody didn't react and stood staring at the boy. Without warning, Melody suddenly clawed for her chain again. But, the boy was too quick and had snatched them out of her reach. Again the girl and the idiot-looking kid fell about laughing. It was then I realised that not only did he look like a donkey with his buckteeth, but he also sounded like one as he sprayed laughter down the alley.

"You've got to be quicker than that!" spotty sneered, his eyes looking wild and excited.

I wanted to spring from my hiding place and tell them to leave the girl alone, but I'd only been above ground an hour or so. What did I really know about these humans? I didn't want to draw any unwanted attention to myself.

Melody grabbed for the chain and again spotty pulled them out of her reach.

"Give it 'ere," donkey-boy said, reaching for the chain. "Let me put it on!"

"Get the fuck outta here!" spotty snapped. "What's wrong with you, Barry? Are you some sorta fag?"

So donkey-boy's name was Barry, huh?

But it was too late, Barry had taken hold of the rosary just as the other boy pulled away. The alleyway came alive with the sound of *clinking* as the chain broke and the tiny beads scattered all over the ground.

"Oh, I'm *so* sorry," spotty smiled, looking back at Melody, who stood and watched the beads bounce and roll away down the alleyway. Her face looked ashen. Melody made a gulping sound in the back of her throat and I wasn't sure if this was an attempt to hold back tears or to try and mask her anger.

"Look what's happened to the pretty necklace," the girl scoffed and again Barry began to bellow like a donkey.

Gripping hold of Melody's hand, spotty stuffed what was left of the broken necklace into it. "You'll forgive me, won't you, holy-girl?" he laughed, and then slapped Melody's cheek hard with the back of his right hand. Looking at his friends, he said, "C'mon, you two."

I watched the three of them skulk away down the alley, making whooping noises and slapping one another across the back. All the while, Melody just stared ahead, her back flat against the wall, her hands knotted by her sides.

When they had gone, Melody bent down onto the knees of her dress and started to gather up the beads. I watched her for a moment or two, not knowing whether I should leave my hiding place or not. Would it bother her if she thought I had seen everything that had happened? Would she be embarrassed? But watching Melody silently crawl along the ground in search of the beads made me feel weird. I felt sad for her. Why? I didn't even know her. She meant nothing to me.

Just watching the plain-looking girl in the plain-looking dress crawling around on all fours wasn't right, and what they had done to her wasn't right, either. So, creeping from behind the rubbish bins, I bent down on all fours and started to gather the beads. They were black in colour and about the same size as peas. Each of them was shiny and had a hole through the middle where they had been attached to the chain. I picked up all that I could find and took them to Melody, who was still on her hands and knees some way down the alleyway.

"Here you go," I said, holding my hand out.

Melody didn't say anything back to me. She didn't even stop searching for the remainder of the beads.

"I've got some of your beads," I told her, and again she said nothing. So placing the beads in a neat pile on the ground, I said, "Suit yourself."

I turned my back on her and walked away.

I made my way back through the town, wondering what else I might see. Not wanting to go too far on my very first day above ground, just in case I couldn't find my way back to the grate in the woods, it wasn't long before I was heading back down the road and out of town. I couldn't be sure of the exact place that I had stepped from in the woods and onto the road, so finding a narrow path on my right, I followed it. Trees stretched up on either side of me, and I wandered slowly, taking in the sounds and the smells that were all new to me. After walking for some time, the trees thinned out and I found myself standing on the shore of a giant lake.

There was a short stretch of sand with an outcrop of rocks that jutted out into the water like a giant finger. I didn't know exactly where I was, but I guessed this was Lake Lure. As I stood on the brown coloured sand, I looked out across the flat, dark surface of the lake and towards a jagged row of mountains in the distance, their peaks flecked with snow.

It was quiet there; I could have been the only person alive. I decided to stay for a while, and sat down on the stretch of sand. As I sat and stared out across the lake, I felt bad for Melody and what had happened to her. Taking a handful of stones, I picked out the smoothest ones and skimmed them across the surface of the lake. And as I watched the last of them bounce across the water, I heard a noise in the trees behind me. Turning, I saw Melody looking back at me from just inside the tree line. At first she startled me, and I wondered what she was doing there. I stood up, brushed the sand from the seat of my trousers, and started to walk away in the opposite direction.

I'd only taken a few steps when I heard her call after me. "Wait! Don't go," she said.

I stopped, and turning, I looked at her.

She stepped clear of the tree line and into the light of the fading sun and made her way up the shore towards me. When she was just a few feet away, Melody put her hands into the deep pocket on the front of her apron. She looked uncomfortable, and a few stringy wisps of hair that had escaped from her bun tossed back and forth in the breeze. She didn't look at me, but idly kicked at the pebbles on the sand.

"So?" I asked, not knowing what to say.

"So what?" she said back without looking up.

"What do you want?"

Then, tilting her head upwards and looking me straight in my eyes, she said, "I wanted to say I was sorry – you know, for what happened back in that alley."

"What have you got to be sorry for?" I asked, confused.

"I was ungrateful," she said. "You helped me pick up the beads from my necklace and I didn't even say thank you."

"Forget it," I shrugged. This was followed by an uneasy silence. Feeling uncomfortable, I added, "I've got to get home." Then turning, I walked away.

I'd only gone a short distance, when I glanced back over my shoulder to see if she was still standing where I'd left her.

Holding my hand in front of my eyes to block out the light from the sunset, I could see that she was now sitting inches from where the water lapped against the shore. Her back was arched and she seemed to be concentrating on something which she had in her hands. Not wanting to leave her all alone, I made my way back up the shoreline towards her.

"What are you doing?" I asked, although I could see she was trying to put the beads back onto the chain that donkey-boy had broken.

"Trying to fix this," Melody said without looking up. Although her hands were small and nimble-looking, I could see she was struggling to get the tiny beads back onto the chain. I sat down next to her on the sand and said, "Let me try."

As if handing over something precious, she handed me the chain and the beads.

"Are these like, religious beads or something?" I asked her, threading the chain through the tiny holes.

"They're called rosary beads," Melody told me, and I could sense she was watching me.

"So you're like, religious then?" I asked, having some knowledge of the humans' belief in a God. As a child I had been told stories about a man called Jesus and how he had died on a cross. The chain that I was mending had a cross.

"I guess," she said back, not taking her eyes off me.

Without looking up from the beads, I said, "You don't sound too sure.'"

"It's not me," she said, then added, "It's my mum who believes in all that stuff."

"Why have you got this chain then?" I asked, turning to look at her, and it was then that I was struck at how blue her eyes actually were.
She continued to stare at me, so I looked away, feeling kinda uncomfortable.

"My mum gave them to me," she said, looking away, as if what she had to tell me was embarrassing. "She says the chain will protect me - keep evil away."

"What, like monsters and stuff?" I asked.

"'The devil' is what she says. My mum reckons that if I

carry the rosary around with me, then no harm will ever come to me - I'll be protected, that sorta thing," she said.

"Those others – the ones who broke your necklace – they obviously don't realise the power of the beads then?" I said, half-smiling. Melody just stared back at me, and at first I wondered if I had offended her by what I'd said. Then a smile formed at the corners of her mouth and she laughed. And when she did, she didn't look so plain after all; her face looked kind of pretty.

"Maybe my mum should tell them," she said.

I fixed the last of the beads onto the chain and handed it back to her. Taking it carefully in her hands so as not to break it again, Melody placed it back into her pocket. Then, looking at me she said, "So what are you doing down here? I thought I was the only one that knew about this place."

"I stumbled across it by accident," I told her.

"Are you new in town?" she asked. "I haven't seen you before. You don't go to school in town."

"I haven't been here very long," I replied, knowing that was a massive understatement, but I couldn't tell her the truth. "I moved into a house just outside of town a few months back with my mother."

"Where about?" she asked.

Jerking my thumb casually over my shoulder, I said, "Over in that direction." Then, wanting to change the subject, I stood up and added, "I should be getting home."

"Are you going to be coming to school?" she asked, getting up.

"Erm, I don't think so," I mumbled. "I don't think we're gonna be in town for long."

"How come?" she asked, and I noticed her pat her apron pocket, as if checking that the rosary beads were still there. It was like she was petrified of losing them. Once Melody had satisfied herself that they were there, she looked at me. "You never answered my question," she said.

"What was that?" I asked right back.

"How come you'll be moving on so soon?" she repeated, and again she fixed her eyes on mine. The bloody red light of the sunset spilled over her head and shoulders, hiding her features in a crimson silhouette.

I didn't say anything back at first. I wasn't sure what to say. Perhaps I should've thought up some kind of cover story before coming above ground. So instead of telling Melody the truth, I shrugged my shoulders and said, "Like you I guess – I do as my mother tells me. If she goes, I follow." Desperate to avoid any more questions, I walked away.

But there was one more question.

"What's your name?" she called out.

"Isidor Smith," I said, glancing back. "And you are?"

"Melody Rose," she said and looked away.

Seizing my chance, I headed up the shore and into the shadows beneath the trees. I wondered if she might follow me, but she didn't. I only looked back once and Melody had gone.

Chapter Eleven

Isidor

I returned up above ground a few days later. My mother had travelled deep into The Hollows to stay with a friend for a week or two, leaving me alone. Left to my own devices and feeling as free as the birds I'd seen in the woods above ground, I returned. This time, though, I didn't head straight into town, I headed for the lake.

Since my last visit, I hadn't been able to stop thinking about what I had seen. I thought of Melody Rose often, and remembering that she had said she spent time at the lake, I secretly hoped that I would find her there. It wasn't that I thought she was hot or anything like that, but she did seem easy to talk to, and I hoped I might find out more about above ground from her.

So with my mother gone, I made my way up through the roots of the tree, into the tunnel, and pushing the grate aside, I found myself back in the woods. It was cold and the ground and the air felt damp. I guessed it had rained recently and I was annoyed that I had missed that. I'd never felt rain against my skin before. Covering the grate with leaves, I made my way through the woods and down to the lake, and there just as I had hoped, sat Melody on the tiny stretch of sand. I couldn't be sure, but it was almost as if she had been waiting for me, because as she looked up, I saw a faint smile cross her lips. I walked along the shoreline and sat beside her. And that's how our friendship started. We became almost inseparable. We spent the next couple of months together, apart from Sunday mornings and Wednesday evenings when Melody's mum took her to church and prayer meetings. I soon came to consider Melody as my best friend. During the first few days of our time spent together, Melody described her mum as being a 'religious nut-nut.'

"What do you mean?" I asked her as we wandered

together through the woods.

"She thinks she's a nun!"

"What, she dresses up as one?" I laughed.

"Kind of, she's not like other mums. She never wears any makeup, her hair is grey and cut short, she only ever wears black, and she always has this large wooden cross hanging around her neck for everyone to see."

"Is that weird?" I asked, not knowing for sure.

"Yeah, that's weird," she said back, straightening the bonnet that she always wore on her head. "My dad left her soon after I was born. If she was anything then like she is now, I don't blame him."

"My father left soon after I was born, too," I told her, but my mother had never said more than that about him. I'd never even seen a picture. "But you sound as if you really hate your mum. I don't hate my mum because my father left us."

"I don't hate her. I just hate the way she is. When she isn't attending church or going to prayer meetings, she spends most of her time in her room."

"What's wrong with that?"

"She's praying. My mum has turned her room into a mini grotto, like the one in Lourdes. She's built this big cave-type thing out of papier-mâché and put a statue of the Virgin Mary in it."

I wasn't sure what a grotto was or anything about a place called Lourdes, but not wanting to appear as if I knew very little about above ground, I cried in disbelief, "Get outter of here! You're kidding me!"

"I'll show you someday," she said, and I noticed a sadness in Melody's eyes that I hadn't seen before. I guessed that maybe she was telling the truth after all about this grotto thing, and a statue of a virgin.

"Is there anything you remember about your father?" Melody asked, bending down and picking up a stone from beneath a huge tree.

"I don't remember anything about him," I told her.

"Nothing at all?" she asked me, toying with the stone in her hands.

"My mother never talks about him," I told her. "I've asked loads of times, but she just changes the subject. I don't even know his name. It's almost as if he didn't really exist at all."

"That's sad," she said softly, and again I saw that look of sadness dance across her eyes. Melody was unique. I had never been able to talk so easily with any of my other friends. I supposed it was because Melody and I had similar backgrounds, but all the same, I thought she was a very sensitive person.

Then, changing the subject I said, "Have you ever seen magic pictures?"

"Magic pictures?" she asked, looking confused.

"A movie projector?" I added, wondering if I'd said the wrong thing.

"The multiplex, is that what you mean?"

"I think so," I said, wishing now that I hadn't said anything. "We call them movie projectors where I come from."

Then, stopping and smoothing the stone with the flat of her hand, she looked at me and said, "Where do you come from, Isidor? You've never said where home is."

"Erm," I stammered. "It's a long way from here."

"What, are you from another country?" Melody asked, sounding more than interested.

"I guess," I said, not knowing what to say next and glancing down at the ground, knowing that my home was some way beneath me.

Then, raising her hand as if to take mine, but changing her mind at the last moment, Melody said, "It doesn't matter to me where you're from, I'm just glad that you came to Lake Lure."

Just wanting to change the subject, I blurted out, "So shall we go to this multiplex and watch Marilyn Monroe?"

"Marilyn Monroe?" Melody said, stifling a giggle. "She doesn't make movies anymore. She's dead and has been for years, way before I was born. Besides, my mum says that movies are sinful, that they fill young people's heads with wicked thoughts."

I thought of what my mother had told me about the hundreds of male Vampyrus leaving The Hollows in search of their own human as beautiful as Marilyn Monroe and said, "Perhaps your mum is right."

We spent the following day mooching around the town. We passed by a shop that was having a new sign painted on it by a man who was high above us on a ladder. At street level, the painter had left a little toolbox rammed with brushes and tiny pots of paint. Before I had a chance to realise what was happening, Melody surprised me by reaching into the toolbox. She grabbed hold of something and then ran off into the maze of narrow alleyways between the shops and houses.

I chased after Melody, her grey dress and apron flowing out behind her. She didn't stop until I had caught up with her by the lake on the outskirts of town.

"What was that all about?" I asked, pretending to be out of breath.

Melody opened her hand, and smiling, she revealed a packet of Marlboro cigarettes.

"What do you want them for?" I asked.

"To smoke, of course! Haven't you ever smoked before?" she smiled at me.

Thinking of the pipe weed that was smoked by some of the elder Vampyrus beneath me, I shook my head and said, "No, why, have you?"

"Once or twice," she replied. "Come on." Melody headed towards a nearby clump of bushes and made her way inside. I looked about, and then followed. Once inside, Melody bent some of the branches back and made a clearing on the floor where we could both sit down. She took two of the cigarettes from the packet and handed one to me. Melody then took a box of matches from the large pocket in the front of her apron and lit one. She popped the cigarette between her lips. I could see the orange flame reflecting in her eyes, and for the first time since meeting her, they looked full of mischief.

Melody sucked on the cigarette and the tip of it glowed orange. I sat and watched her as blue smoke squirted from her nostrils. She seemed to be an expert and I guessed she had done this many times before. Melody lit one for me, and without thinking, I popped the cigarette into my mouth and inhaled. I was instantly struck by the hot smoke in the back of my throat and I coughed it back out, my eyes watering. Melody giggled and said, "You haven't tried this before, have you?"

I shook my head and waited for the woozy feeling that I now had to clear. I watched Melody as she thoughtfully puffed away and I let my cigarette burn almost to the butt before I tried another puff. Melody was an enigma to me. On one hand she was this really sensitive person who would talk honestly and openly about her feelings, but on the other, she was someone who lived in fear of breaking the rules that her mum made her live by. But as I sat and watched her, dressed in her bonnet, grey dress and apron, with a cigarette dangling from the corner of her mouth, I realised she also had this darker, mischievous side. What I couldn't come to understand about my own feelings, was that I was drawn equally to both sides of her personality.

Chapter Twelve

Isidor

Melody and I spent almost every day together. We would regularly visit our makeshift camp in the bushes down by the lake, and by now I had become quite an accomplished smoker. We would spend the warmer days lying on our backs, boots off, our feet being caressed by the cool water of the lake, enjoying a leisurely smoke or two.

Both Melody and I were keen to keep away from home. Me, because my mother was away and I wanted to snatch the opportunity to come above ground as much as possible. But I soon wondered if my true reason for wanting to come above ground wasn't to discover what the world above me was really like, but to see and spend as much time as I could with Melody.

Melody had a different reason. Her mother, although she never neglected Melody materially, she did starve her emotionally. Melody described a picture of her home life as being a 'Religious Hell.' She wasn't allowed to listen to music, unless it was classical or gospel and she couldn't put pictures of her favourite rock stars or any movie star on her bedroom wall. Her mum monitored what she read and Melody told me how she had gone berserk when her mum had found a copy of *Shrine* by James Herbert under her mattress.

"She took it into the backyard and set fire to it. I wouldn't have minded but it wasn't even mine, I'd borrowed it from the library!" Melody said. "I remember her coming home one day and finding me watching MTV."

"What did she do?" I asked.

"She unplugged the television there and then, and we haven't had one in the house since. She told me that it was 'devil' music and that it would corrupt my soul. My mum then went on to add that if I hadn't have been born, she could have been a nun."

I felt terrible for Melody as she told me this. I could only imagine how much this must have hurt her. To offer some comfort I said, "You know, she probably didn't mean that."

Then, just when I thought Melody was going to open up to me, she said, "I don't want to talk about her anymore," then she lit another smoke.

So we spent lazy days stretched out on the bank of the lake, smoking, and being caressed by the cool evening breeze that meandered around the trees and our secret camp. We wouldn't leave until the sun had made its way across the sky and disappeared behind the mountains that framed the lake before us, leaving the water bathed in an orange glow. We would sit together, motionless, lost in the beauty of the spectacle before us. As dusk began to fall, and the shadows of the trees grew tall and dark and stretched across the lake, we would hide the cigarettes in our camp, then slowly walk away, leaving the lake to the night. I would walk Melody through the woods, and once on the road, we would go our separate ways. I would watch Melody disappear into the distance then I'd sneak back into the woods and climb back into the hole, covering it with the grate. Our days never got much more exciting than that, until the day Melody didn't show up at the lake.

A few weeks after meeting Melody, I arrived early that Saturday morning at the lake. It had been particularly cold that day and I had wrapped up warm with several layers of clothing. I waited on the shore for Melody to arrive. As I stood and stomped my feet into the sand, I puffed warm mouthfuls of breath over my freezing hands. I waited the entire morning for Melody to turn up. In the end, I gave up and headed into town.

Melody had often told me that she liked to read, and after hearing the story of how her mum had destroyed that book, I decided to go to the place that Melody had called the library. I knew that I could take a book from there without needing money, as Melody explained how you could take books home for free. I made my way through the town, which was pretty quiet due to the freezing wind. In the town square, I found the building that Melody had pointed out to me, and I climbed the grey stone steps and went through the double wooden doors.

Just like the streets outside, the aisles between the huge rows of books were quiet. I passed between them, looking at all the brightly coloured covers. I ran my fingers along the spines, and I picked up several and fanned the pages beneath my nose. They had a musty old smell which was wonderful. I continued amongst the rows of books, until I found one that had a beautiful red rose on the front. Melody's surname was Rose, so guessing that she might like the cover, and knowing that I could borrow books for free from the library, I placed the book inside my coat.

I made my way out of the library, climbed down the steps and started off across the town square, heading back towards the lake. About halfway across the square, I heard someone shout.

"Hey, you!"

I stopped and turned around and looked in the direction of the voice. Sitting on the back of a wooden bench were the three teenagers I had seen bullying Melody in the alleyway.

"Hey, you!" the spotty dude called out again, and donkey-boy sprayed laughter.

I turned my back on them and headed across the square. Almost at once, I heard the sound of feet running behind me. Looking back, I could see spotty dude, donkey-boy, and the girl coming after me. Instead of running, I stood my ground.

"What do you want?" I asked as they gathered around me.

"Haven't seen you around town before," the girl said, and up close she looked too pretty to be hanging around with these two idiots. Her skin was pale with a cluster of light brown freckles across the bridge of her nose and cheeks.

Before I'd the chance to say anything, spotty dude said, "What's your name?"

"Isidor," I said.

"Isidor?" he sneered. "What sort of a fag name is that?"

Hearing this, donkey-boy sprayed laughter again, a

stringy coil of spit swinging from his buckteeth.

"My name is Isidor," I said again, not understanding what was so funny.

"Isidor," the girl whispered, staring at me. *"Isidorable!"*

I don't think spotty dude liked the way the girl was looking at me. He grunted, and then gripped my coat in his fist. "Nice coat," he said.

"Let go of me," I told him, fearing that if he somehow managed to take my coat, they would see those purple scars running down the inside of my arms.

"Give me the coat," spotty boy barked, gripping it now with both hands.

"No," I insisted. "Leave me alone."

"Leave me alone," donkey-boy mimicked in a whiney voice, then started to laugh again.

"Let's see your muscles," the girl chipped in, and I detected excitement in her voice. I don't think it was seeing me being ribbed that excited her.

"Yeah, let's see your muscles, you fag," spotty dude shouted and this time, he yanked so hard on my coat, that the buttons came away. The sound of them clinking onto the ground reminded me of Melody's beads falling from her broken chain.

Not wanting to get into a fight with them – I didn't want to hurt them – I tried to pull away, but the boy's grip on me was firm. I spun around, and as I did, my right arm slipped from my coat sleeve. At once I heard the girl gasp as she looked at my arm. Although I wore a T-shirt, you could clearly see my arm and the fierce-looking scar that ran up from the crook of my elbow. Although her eyes were wide open, she didn't scream. It was then that I realised she hadn't noticed my scars – not yet anyway – she was too mesmerised by something else.

"Wow," she murmured in wonder.

Although I was only fourteen, my arms were very muscular. Most male Vampyrus were built like me – it was just the way we were made.

As the girl stood and stared at me, spotty dude shouted at her and said, "Don't just stand there, Lucy, help take his coat."

"Yeah, let's take his coat," donkey-boy sniggered with a feverish excitement as he begun to tug at the other sleeve. With both of them on me, they pulled my coat free.

"Give it back," I said, as spotty boy put it on.

"How do I look?" he asked, turning around in front of Lucy.

"You look good, Ray," she said, keeping one eye on me.

Then, from behind us, I heard a whooping sound. I turned around to see a police car pulling up at the kerb. Then, at the very same moment, I heard a woman shouting.

I looked back over my shoulder to see a lady running down the library steps and across the square towards us.

"Officer! Officer!" she shouted. "That boy stole a book."

By the time I'd looked back again, the door to the police car was open and a giant of a man in a smart blue uniform was climbing out.

Seeing him, donkey-boy screeched, "Let's split!" and I watched him and Lucy race away.

Ray was slower to make his escape, and before he had even managed two steps, the police officer had taken hold of the collar of my coat, which Ray was now wearing.

"Well, well, well," the officer grunted. "Raymond Baines – I might have known."

"I haven't done anything wrong," Ray groaned, as he tried to work his way free of my coat.

"It was him!" the lady said, pointing at Ray. "I know it was him who stole the book because he was wearing that big long coat."

"I haven't stolen any book," Ray protested, his spotty face glowing redder than before.

"Empty your pockets," the officer shouted, his voice so deep that it sounded like thunder.

I stood there quietly, my arms folded across my chest as I tried to hide my scars. Ray flinched at the sound of the officer's voice, then reached inside the coat. With his eyes widening, he pulled out the book with the rose on the front from within my coat.

"That's the book," the woman insisted, pushing her glasses back onto the bridge of her nose.

"Give it back to the librarian, you thief!" the officer roared at Ray.

"But I didn't steal it," Ray protested, handing her the book.

"A thief and a liar," the officer barked. "What is your father going to say this time? The shame that you have brought upon that poor man, a military man as well. And your mother – what is she going to say? This is the third time in a month that I've had to take you home."

"But I didn't steal it," Ray said. Then, jabbing a finger in my direction he said, "He took it."

As if noticing me for the first time, the police officer glared at me and said, "Who are you?"

"Isidor," I said, guessing that Melody had been mistaken about the whole borrowing from the library thing.

"Isidor who?" the officer snapped.

"Isidor Smith," I told him.

"And from which rock have you climbed out from?"

"Oh, no I haven't climbed out from beneath any rock," I said staring at him. Did he know that I'd come from below ground? So I quickly added, "It was more like a hole..."

But before I'd had the chance to explain, the officer said, "Right, wise guy, get into the car, I'm taking you home." Then, looking at Ray, he added, "both of you!"

With my heart beginning to race, I climbed into the back of the police car. Ray followed me. He was quiet and I could see that his usually bright red face was now pale and sick-looking. What was he so scared about? I had every reason to fear being taken home by this police officer – it could be very interesting.

The giant cop wedged himself behind the wheel and started the car. It rolled away from the kerb and the sensation felt kind of strange. Wait until the others in The Hollows hear about this. I was actually traveling in a car, and not any ordinary car – a police car with big red and blue flashing lights and a siren. Cool!

"I'll take you home first," the cop said, glaring back at Ray. "I'm sick and tired of having to look at your stupid face."

Ray ignored him and looked out of the window as the world flashed past. I noticed that he wrung his hands nervously in his lap. We hadn't been moving for very long when the cop slowed the car, turned up a narrow lane, and stopped outside a house set back from the road.

"Out!" the officer barked.

Following Ray, I climbed from the back of the car. The house was surrounded by a tidy front garden and a white wooden fence with a gate in it. A path led up to the polished front door. I followed. Ray walked ahead of me. He was quiet now, his head slumped forward.

Before the cop had even rapped on the door with his huge knuckles, it flew open to reveal a thick-set man. He stood with his back straight and shoulders back. He was dressed in smart black trousers and a pale blue shirt. His greying hair was combed immaculately back off his brow and he had a neatly trimmed moustache beneath his broad nose.

He glared over the cop's shoulder at Ray, then back at the cop.

"What's he done now,, Constable Freeman?"

"Stealing from the library," the officer explained.

Looking at his son with a grim stare, Ray's father said in an icy voice, "You are a disgrace. Now get inside."

With his head still resting against his chest, as if unable to meet his father's frozen stare, Ray slipped past him and into the house.

"I am so sorry, Constable Freeman. I am deeply ashamed of what has happened," Ray's father said.

"It's the third time this month that I've had to bring your son..."

"I can promise it will be the last, Constable," Ray's father said, rolling back his shoulders and puffing out his chest. Then as if wanting to change the subject, he looked at me and said, "And who might you be?"

"Says his name is Isidor Smith," the officer answered for me.

"And were you stealing books?" Ray's father asked me.

"Erm, no – I don't think so," I said, knowing that I had taken the library book but just to borrow it.

"I don't think he is the sharpest tool in the box," Constable Freeman said, looking at Ray's father.

Then, the officer's radio began to make a squawking noise and a cracked and garbled voice started to come from it. Constable Freeman snatched the radio from his belt and held it to his ear. With his brow becoming a series of creases, he looked at me and said, "It's your lucky day, sunshine. There's been a fatal crash up on the main road – you'll have to make your own way home." Then, placing his radio back onto his belt, he leaned into my face and breathed, "Be warned, boy, don't ever let me catch you pricking about in my town again."

"Yes," I said, lowering my head.

Then he was gone, running back down the garden path and wedging himself back behind the wheel of his car. In a blaze of flashing lights and screaming sirens, he sped away. I looked back at the house and Ray's father was staring at me.

"Get out of here," he ordered and slammed the door on me.

I made my way back down the path. It was as I reached the front gate, I realised that Ray still had my coat. I would need that. I had a long walk back to the woods and I didn't want the humans to see that I was different. I wanted to hide my arms. So, turning around, I headed back up the garden path. I reached the front door and just as I was about to knock, I heard shouting come from inside. The voice sounded so angry, that it made my blood chill in my veins.

With my back hunched, I climbed into the flowerbeds that ran alongside the house, and crept around the side. Hidden from view, I slowly eased myself up into a crouching position and peered through a window set into the side of the house and I was so shocked by what I saw, that I ducked my head down again. With my heart racing in my chest like a trip hammer, I took a deep breath and peered back through the window again.

Ray was standing in the middle of the room, which was

well furnished with comfy-looking chairs and expensive-looking pictures on the walls. There was a cabinet fastened to the far wall and it had a collection of guns in it.

For some reason, Ray had stripped naked, apart from a pair of blue boxer shorts that hung from his narrow hips. Just like his face, a spattering of sore-looking pimples covered his chest and bony shoulders. His father stood before him, tall and straight, and he had something in his hands. From my hiding place, I could see the fear in Ray's eyes as he looked front at his father.

"Listen in, boy! Listen in!" His father said in that voice that would have frozen the warmest of hearts. "You are a disgrace. Do you have any idea of the position that I hold in this town? Do you have any idea of the respect that I command? I fought in the desert for boys like you. In fact, I fought alongside boys not much older than you. But unlike you, they were men. You're pathetic. You disgust me."

"I'm sorry, sir" Ray mumbled, and I saw his legs wobble as if he were going to fall over or faint.

"What did you say, boy?" his father screeched, his voice sounding nasally and high-pitched.

"It wasn't me, sir," Ray pleaded with him. "I didn't steal that book."

"Don't lie to me, boy! You know what will happen to you if I find out that you've lied to me?"

"No, sir," Ray replied even though I suspected Ray knew very well what was coming. The fear I could see in his eyes told me that.

"I'll tell you what will happen. You'll be having a meeting with Mr. Persuader! You know who Mr. Persuader is, don't you, boy?" his father hissed, their noses now just inches apart.

"No, sir," I heard Ray say.

His father then brought into view a large rubber sole which looked as if it had been removed from a pair of sneakers. He slapped it repeatedly against the open palm of his hand in front of Ray's face.

"Do you know why this is called Mr. Persuader, boy?" he

asked.

"No, sir," Ray whispered, his bottom lip trembling.

"Because with the help of Mr. Persuader, I could *persuade* you to do anything for me, boy!" his father seemed to gloat with excitement.

I cringed at the thought of what he might have had in mind as he stared at Ray with his hard, grey eyes.

"Now get upstairs so I can punish you before your mother gets home," he barked.

Without saying anything, and with the look of acceptance in his eyes, Ray silently turned and walked slowly from the room. His father followed, Mr. Persuader swinging from his fist. When they had gone, I crept away from the window and made my way back down the road with a sinking feeling in my heart and a sickness in my stomach.

Chapter Thirteen

Isidor

I stepped off the road and into the woods. Part of me wanted to go home, back to The Hollows. I had seen enough and I couldn't get those images of Ray cowering in his boxer shorts before his father out of my head. He seemed a completely different person to the one I had seen hurting Melody and the person who had stolen my coat. But it wasn't just Ray and his father that I couldn't get from my head – it was Melody, too. What had happened to her today? Why hadn't she turned up at the lake?

Wondering – or was that secretly hoping – that she might be there, I headed away from the hole in the ground that led home and started through the woods to the lake. I sat alone on the sandy shore, and as the white winter sun touched the edge of the lake on the horizon, and the water took on the appearance of black coloured velvet, I heard a rustle in the trees behind me. The sound was so sudden in the stillness of the approaching evening, that I jumped to my feet, half expecting to see that cop once again. To my relief it was Melody who appeared from within the dense foliage. My delight at seeing her was short-lived, and my sense of annoyance at having to wait for her the entire morning raced to the fore. Melody must have sensed my irritation, as before she had even reached me, she was offering an apology.

"Isidor, I'm sorry."

"I waited all morning! I was freezing, Melody!" I moaned. "Where were you?"

"I'm really sorry," she said, gently placing a hand on my forearm. "You are cold."

"So you gonna tell me what you've been up to?" I asked her.

"Your ears are almost purple!" she tried to joke and change the subject all at the same time.

"What do you expect; it must be at least three below zero out here, and stop changing the subject!" I moaned.

"Aw, c'mon, I've said I'm sorry, haven't I?" she half-smiled at me, and when she did, her face looked real pretty.

"It's not the fact that I was left waiting in the cold. I ran into Ray and his friends and they stole my coat."

"He stole your coat?" she gasped. "Poor Isidor. No wonder you're so cold." Then, she came forward and gently wrapped her arms around me as if trying to warm me. I met her gaze and those blue eyes of hers glistened in the cold. It was impossible to be angry with her. "Do you want to talk about it?" she smiled.

"I should be getting home," I said, feeling a little uncomfortable as she held me. It wasn't that I didn't like her holding me – it felt nice – and that's what made me feel uncomfortable.

"You can stay awhile, can't you?" she pleaded, looking up into my eyes. "I don't want to go home just yet. Mother is there, but she will be going to a prayer meeting later. Stay with me a little while. I've got some cigarettes."

"I don't want to smoke," I told her. "I don't like it. But I'll stay with you if you really want me to."

"I really want you to," she said, taking my hand and leading me up the shore to our camp.

The thick bushes and branches offered some protection against the chilly wind that blew in off the lake. Taking a box of matches from her apron, Melody bunched together a small pile of dry leaves and twigs and lit a small fire. Huddled together, we warmed ourselves in front of it. I crossed my arms over my chest to hide those scars. As the smoke circled up from the fire in a thin stream, I told Melody about my adventure. It felt kinda magical to be sitting beside her in front of the fire because at last I was telling a story and that's something I'd always wanted to do. Just like all good storytellers, I made up my own ending. I didn't tell Melody what I had seen through the window of Ray's house. I didn't think it would be right or fair. Not because I owed Ray any favours, but because I wasn't meant to have seen that. That was Ray's secret.

"So you got into all that trouble because you went to get me a book?" she said, pushing a loose piece of hair back under her bonnet.

"Yes," I said, watching her light a cigarette.

"Why?" she asked, looking confused.

"Because you said that your mum threw your other book into the fire," I explained.

"What was the book about?" she asked me, blowing smoke from the corner of her mouth.

"It had a rose on the front."

"Okay," she said with a curious frown. "So what was it called?"

"I don't know," I told her and looked into the fire – anything so I didn't have to stare into her eyes. "I just got it because it had a rose on the front – just like your name."

"So you don't know what the book was about or what it was called," she giggled.

"Are you laughing at me?" I whispered, not taking my eyes off the flames.

"Well, it's kind of a dumb thing to do, don't you think?" she giggled again. "Who would choose a book if they didn't know what it was called or what it..."

"You're just like the rest of them," I moaned.

"Sorry?" she said, her smile fading.

"You think I'm stupid, just like the others do – my friends back home. Yet they're not really my friends." Then, turning to face her, I added, "Real friends don't call you stupid because you can't read or write."

As if realising the mistake she had made, Melody's mouth dropped open, and she said, "Oh my God, Isidor, I didn't realise. You didn't know what the book was about because you couldn't read the title, could you?"

"No," I whispered, looking back into the fire. "So now you know, I'm thick, stupid, a joke."

Melody threw her cigarette into the fire and gently placed her hand on my shoulder. "I don't think you're stupid," she whispered.

"No?" I snapped. "So what do you think?"

"I think you are the sweetest guy that I've ever met," she said, gently placing her hand against my cheek and turning my face towards her. "You are the only person in this town who doesn't avoid me because of the way my mother makes me dress. Even the people in church keep away from us. No one dresses the way we do. You didn't judge me, Isidor, and I'm not judging you. You helped me mend my necklace, you went and chose a book for me – it had a rose on it just like my name. No one has ever done anything like that for me."

"Why did you laugh then?" I asked, looking into her eyes.

"Because I wanted to cry, but I just couldn't let it show," she whispered and looked away.

"Why did you want to cry?" I asked softly.

"Because I just can't stop hurting....that is..." she trailed off.

"What?" I pushed gently. "What stops you hurting, Melody?"

"You do, Isidor," she said. "When I'm with you, I stop thinking."

"Thinking about what?"

Then, taking my hand in hers, she stood up and said, "Come with me and I'll show you."

Melody led me through the fading daylight. Both of us bent forward against the cold, icy wind that had crept up and twisted itself around the streets. It was gone eight p.m. and the town had closed down for the night. We were the only people on the streets apart from the occasional car which drove slowly past, the tyres crunching over the cobbled roads.

"Where are you taking me?" I asked her.

"Home," she said, not letting go of my hand.

"Will your mum mind me coming over?"

"She won't know. She's at a prayer meeting tonight."

Although I had never met Melody's mother and I only had the snippets of information that she had told me about her, I still felt incredibly apprehensive about going to her home. Even though I knew she wouldn't be there, I couldn't help but get cramps in my stomach with nerves. Just as we reached the outskirts of town, Melody took a sudden turn to the right off the main road and led me up a narrow track and into the darkness. We walked silently in the dark for several minutes, until I could just make out the shape of a squat-looking house on the horizon. Melody steered me towards this and I guessed it was her home. The sudden sound of a startled bird screeched and flapped its wings against the night as it soared out of the trees that lined the path on either side of us. I jumped.

"Jeezus, Isidor! I'm meant to be the girl here," Melody laughed nervously.

I could sense that she felt anxious, but I suspected it wasn't the dark or our current surroundings that made her feel like this, but the act of taking me back to her home for the first time and whatever it was that she wanted to show me.

Melody's house sat in a small plot of land which was surrounded by a waist-high wooden fence. She swung open the gate which whined on its frozen hinges and led me across the front yard to the porch. Although it was dark, and the moonlight only shone intermittently through passing clouds, I could see that Melody's home from the outside looked well-kept. It was only when Melody pushed open the front door and flipped on the hallway light that I immediately got the feeling something was odd about it.

"Holy moly!" I whispered through my teeth as I stepped inside and looked around in bewilderment. The short hallway was covered in an array of pictures, twelve in all. Like I've already said, I knew a little about the man named Jesus, and each of these pictures was of him. They weren't beautiful pictures, they were ugly. They depicted him suffering in a way that I hadn't contemplated before when I had heard stories about him. In each picture, he had been drawn in a skeletal and emaciated fashion. His eyes looked odd, and it was only as I stared at them, I realized they had been penned deliberately to look too big for his face. This gave him an almost alien-looking quality, which I found haunting. These were in stark contrast to paintings that I had seen of Jesus before, in books brought down to The Hollows by those who had adventured above ground. Those books had illustrations of him with a loving smile, locks of honey coloured hair, and angel-blue eyes.

"This way," Melody whispered, her voice dragging me out of the weird trance the pictures had placed me in. Beneath the stairs there was a door which Melody opened. I peered over her shoulder and could see a set of wooden stairs leading down into darkness.

"I'll show you what's down here," she whispered, making her way down into the pitch black. I silently followed. I held onto a rough feeling banister with my left hand and held my other directly out in front of me. The stairs cried out beneath us as we placed our weight on them. At the bottom, my hand struck Melody on the shoulder as she suddenly came to a halt in front of me. For a moment there was silence, stillness, nothing. Then I heard a 'click' as Melody pulled on the light switch which hung from the ceiling just above us. My new surroundings appeared dimly before me in the murky glow of the naked light bulb.

My throat made a shallow wheezing sound as I sucked in a mouthful of air in complete shock at what had just been revealed to me. The basement had been turned into a tiny chapel. The smell of melted candles and incense hung heavy in the air. There were two small pews in front of an altar which had been covered with a crimson cloth. There were rows of candles down the length of each wall, and at the end of the rows there was a large statue of Jesus. Positioned behind the altar was a huge cross which hung about four foot from the floor and protruded by about a foot from the wall.

"This place is creepy," I whispered.

"It's where my mum locks me away," she said softly.

"What?" I couldn't understand what she had just said to me.

"When I was a kid, if I was bad, she would bring me down here. I had to stay for hours, sometimes days, kneeling on that little box," she said, pointing to a small crate at the foot of the cross.

"Get out of here!" I breathed.

Melody stared at me without replying. I looked into her

eyes and that brilliant blue had faded. My stomach lurched with a sickening feeling and I knew that she was telling the truth.

"Why?" I tried to find the right words.

Melody settled into one of the small pews, and in a hushed and broken voice, she told me everything.

"Mum would drag me down here and make me strip to my underwear, and all the time she would be praying...almost chanting. She would rant over and over again. Her face would look as if in pain and I remember seeing spit form like foam around her mouth. She would keep me locked down here for days at a time." Melody looked in the direction of the cross on the wall and I followed her gaze.

"Sometimes I would have to kneel on the crate for so long that my knees would bleed."

"Why would she do that to you?" I asked, stunned at what she was telling me.

"Because she said I had an evil demon living within me. She would make me fast, too. My mum said she was starving the demon out of me."

"How long would she make you go without food?" I gasped.

"Until I could take no more," Melody explained. "My stomach would start to cramp and all I would be able to think about was food and water. My thirst was so bad sometimes, the pain was unbearable."

"Where would your mum go while you were left starving down here in the dark?"

"She would sit right here and pray for my forgiveness. Sometimes, I could hear her sobbing hysterically."

"When would she let you eat?"

"When I was near unconsciousness," Melody said, looking up at the cross, her face haunted as she remembered the torture her mum had put her through. "I used to hallucinate due to the pain in my stomach and throat. I could hear water rushing past me, then drowning me. But it didn't bring me any closer to God, like my mum hoped it would. It just made me believe there was no such thing. If there were a God, he wouldn't have let me suffer like that. I would finally rock forward on the crate, my knees red and raw, close to exhaustion. It was like I was falling into a well of blackness, but before I hit the bottom, my mum would catch me in her arms."

I put my arm around Melody's shoulder and hugged her as we sat on the pew and she stared up at that cross.

"Melody, I've never heard anything like that before. I don't know what to say. You've got to report this, she can't do this to you," I whispered.

"Who would believe me? I'm not sure that even you do."

"I believe you; it's just that I can't believe that any mum could do that to their kid." But then I thought of what I had seen through Ray's window and wasn't quite so sure.

"Well, believe it or not, she does treat me like that and has always done so!" she insisted.

"Haven't you got anyone else, family that you could go and live with?" I asked.

"No," she said, shaking her head. "Anyway, she hasn't locked me down here for a while."

I studied Melody's profile in the dim light of the makeshift chapel, and for a fourteen-year-old, she looked tired and haunted.

As if knowing what I was thinking, Melody stood up and said, "C'mon, the tour isn't over yet!" Throwing the chapel into darkness once more, she led me up the stairs and to her mother's bedroom.

Melody swung open the door, and her mum's room was warmly lit with two red coloured light bulbs that sat in shaded lamps. Like the hall and so much of the house, the room was decorated with haunting pictures of Jesus at various stages of his crucifixion. The room was sparsely furnished with a single bed, a dark wooden wardrobe, and a reading chair. The most dominant feature in the room was the papier-mâché grotto Melody's mother had constructed in the far corner of the room. If it hadn't have been for its bizarre location, it would have been a truly impressive piece of work. It was very detailed, and from a distance, it did look like an actual stone structure. It had been painted, and a great deal of time and effort had been taken to paint plant life and flowers all around its base, and what appeared to be wild ivy growing up the length of one side. The front of the structure had been hollowed out and in this stood the most beautiful statue of a woman who I figured had to be Mary, Jesus's mother. Unlike the many pictures of Jesus which were hanging around the house, this was truly breathtaking. In the statue's hands she held a set of rosary beads just like the ones that Melody carried in the pocket on the front of her apron.

"What do you make of that?" Melody asked. She was whispering again.

"I've never seen anything like it in my life," I murmured, moving forward to get a closer look. "What's the point of it?" I asked.

"I don't know," Melody sighed. "I think it's meant to resemble this holy place in France – Lourdes."

"Wouldn't it have been easier to buy a plane ticket and visit the place for real?" I half joked.

"If you were normal, yeah. But we're not talking about your everyday pilgrim, are we?" Melody said.

"What would your mum do if she knew we had been in here?" I asked, continuing to study her abnormal handiwork.

"To her it would be like one of us taking a leak on God's robes!"

I turned away from the grotto and was just about to say, *I think I should be going*, when we heard it: the unmistakable sound of someone's footsteps coming up the stairs.

Chapter Fourteen

Isidor

We looked at each other. Even in the glow of the red lights in the room, I could see that the entire colour had drained from Melody's face and she looked petrified.

"She's back!" Melody whispered.

"What are we going to do?" I panicked. I could see Melody's eyes frantically search the room for somewhere for both of us to hide. Outside, I could hear her mum's footsteps and they were getting closer.

"In the wardrobe" she breathed in my ear.

"Are you kidding me?" I whispered back.

"Get inside," she hissed, opening the wardrobe door. I could see real fear in her eyes and sense it in her voice.

Before I had the chance to say anything else, Melody pushed me in the back and into the wardrobe. The clothes on the hangers smelt musty and old as they brushed against my arms and face. Melody squeezed herself in next to me and closed the door. My heart was racing so fast I thought it was going to explode out of my chest. I stood as still as possible and I hoped that Melody's mum wasn't going to bed for the night. I knew that I wouldn't be able to hide in here until morning.

It wasn't completely dark in the wardrobe, and I noticed a chink of light seeping in through a gap in the door. As quietly as I could, I crouched and pressed my eye against the gap. I saw Melody's mum enter the room and close the door behind her. I couldn't see all of her, just brief glimpses, but enough to know that she dressed just the same as Melody.

How did I get myself into this? I cursed.

Then her mum stopped in the middle of the room, and I saw her take off her bonnet and apron.

Oh my God, she is going to bed! I'm trapped! I screamed inside.

She rummaged around for something in the grotto, and

then dropped to her knees. Her head was cast forward so I couldn't see her face. But in her hands she held a set of beads, just like the ones Melody had. I guessed that's what her mum had taken from the statue in the grotto.

How did I get into this? I thought again.

Then her mum started to speak as if she was having a conversation with someone else in the room, whom I couldn't see.

"Forgive me," she muttered, head resting against her hands which were clasped before her. "Please take the burden which is my daughter from me."

Melody must have heard what her mother had said, as she moved uncomfortably beside me.

"I know that I sinned, that I was tempted by the devil," her mother continued. "But he tricked me into falling in love with him. He used me to carry his demon."

I closed my eyes because if I did, it meant that perhaps I wasn't hiding in the wardrobe and having to listen to this woman speaking about my friend in such a way.

"Once he had placed his demon inside of me, he left," her mum continued to mumble. "But I know he will return one day. That's why you must help me rid my daughter of her demon."

Holding my breath, and turning as quietly as I could, I looked at Melody. She cowered in the corner of the wardrobe. In the chink of light that cut through the gap in the door, I could see tears glistening in her eyes. I pulled her close to me, then resting my forehead against hers I gently placed my hands over her ears so she didn't have to hear what her mum was saying about her.

Her mum continued to babble her wicked prayers on the other side of the wardrobe door. To block out the sound of her voice, in my head I pictured Melody and me down by the lake, our feet being covered by the cool water that lapped against the shore. With our foreheads touching, I hoped somehow Melody would see those pictures too. I closed my eyes and pictured her.

It was like I completely lost track of time. I could no

89

longer hear Melody's mum praying. Taking my hands from over Melody's ears, I shuffled around on the spot and peered through the gap.

I watched as Melody's mum placed the beads back in the statue's hand, and then headed for the bedroom door. Here she took off her plain grey dress and let it flutter to the floor. With her back to me, I was horrified to see her back was criss-crossed with a network of old scars. They were silver-looking in the red glow of the lamps. She took a dressing gown from the back of the door, wrapped herself in it, and left the room.

No sooner had she gone, than Melody was pushing me from the wardrobe. She tiptoed across the room towards the door.

"*C'mon!*" I could sense the panic in her voice.

"Is it safe for us to come out now?" I asked.

"She'll be having a shower. *C'mon!*" Melody pulled at my arm and we snuck from her mother's room. We crept along the landing and as we passed the bathroom, I could hear the sound of running water. I just wanted to get out of there and I began to descend the stairs two at a time. In my haste, I lost my footing and clattered into Melody who fell forward and tumbled down the last few stairs.

"Melody! Melody *is that you?*" her mother called out from the bathroom.

Melody clambered to her feet and dragged me to the front door.

"Who's there? Melody is that you?" her mother called again.

I looked back momentarily and saw a shadow spill across the wall at the top of the stairs. Melody yanked open the front door and pushed me outside onto the porch.

I looked at her as she stood in the doorway. "Come with me, Melody. I can take you home with me – it's different – but better than here."

"I can't," she said.

"Melody! Melody! Who are you talking to? *Who's there?*" her mum called again from the top of the stairs.

"It's okay, mum. It's just me," Melody called back.

"Please, Melody, come with me?" I begged in a hushed tone. It was then I finally saw the tears she said she had been unable to cry earlier. They seeped from the corner of each eye and spilled onto her cheeks.

"I can't come with you, Isidor," she said, shutting the door.

Chapter Fifteen

Isidor

The next day I was anxious to meet up with Melody, I was worried for her, and I didn't like the idea of leaving her there, not after what I'd seen and heard the previous night. I hadn't slept well, deep within The Hollows. The images of what I had seen kept going around in my mind. Humans seemed to be so cruel to one another. It didn't seem to matter who they were or where they came from. My mother was right, though; they were all the same in a way. Melody's mum thought she was a holy person, but was very cruel. Ray's father had been a solider – a brave man – and wanted the respect of others, but he was cruel to his son, too.

Relieved to see Melody waiting for me, I walked towards her, and as we mooched through the woods towards the lake on that bright, winter's morning, Melody said, "You won't ever tell anyone what you saw and heard at my house, will you?"

"I can't believe you have to ask me that," I said back.

"I know I can trust you, but I would hate for anybody else to find out."

"Well they won't find out from me. I promise," I assured her. And that was that, the subject was never mentioned again, but it was always one that would play on my mind.

Melody had a rucksack with her that day, she had smuggled it from home and bought it down to the lake. Placing the rucksack on the ground just outside our camp, Melody took a beat-up looking radio from it.

"I thought we could listen to some music," she said.

I could remember what she had told me about her mother and her dislike of pop music. I sensed that Melody, in her own secretive way, was starting to rebel. I watched her turn the silver coloured dial on top of the radio until music came from the speaker. I didn't know the name of the song at the time, but it was played a lot by the radio stations and Melody and I would often sit by the lake and sing along. I later discovered the song was called *Heroes* by David Bowie. As I sat looking at her, dressed in those plain and old fashioned looking clothes, I noticed something different about her eyes.

"Are you wearing makeup?" I asked.

"Yeah, do you like it?" she smiled, looking pleased that I had noticed.

"Well...I s'pose..." I started. "What would your mother say?"

"She won't find out," Melody said and took a lipstick from the bag.

It was bright red, and she covered her lips with it. As I sat and watched her, I asked, "Where did you get the makeup from?"

"From a shop," she smiled, glancing at me. Then, patting the big pouch on the front of her apron, she added, "Comes in real handy for slipping things in."

"You stole that makeup?" I asked, again surprised by her.

"Just like you and the library book," she winked at me, and secretly I thought she looked prettier without the lipstick and the black stuff around her eyes. I wasn't going to say anything, though, as she seemed to like it and that was cool with me.

"Speaking of books," Melody added, "I've got something for you."

Again, I watched as she reached into the bag and this time she produced a comic book.

"Why have you got me a book?" I asked. "You know I can't read."

"But I can," she smiled at me, "and I'm gonna teach you."

"What's it called?" I asked, feeling scared at the thought of making a fool of myself in front of her.

Holding up the book, Melody said, "It's called *The Incredible Hulk.*"

I looked at the shiny cover of the comic book and could see a big, green, angry monster on the front with colourful writing splashed across it – but to me they were just shapes. "What's it about?"

"This dude – his name is Bruce Banner but he leads a secret life," she started to explain, thumbing to the first page. "Everyone thinks he's like, a regular guy, but really he's a monster. He can't tell anyone, because if people find out they..."

"Would capture him, put him in a cage, then open him up to see how he worked," I cut in.

"Pretty much," Melody said, eyeing me. "How did you know that?"

"It was just something my mum tried to explain to me once," I told her, thinking of my wings hidden behind those scars. "People don't like *different*, do they?"

Glancing down at her dress, the apron, and thick workman-like boots on her feet, Melody whispered, "I guess not." Then, as if wanting to change the subject, she waved the comic in the air and said, "Am I gonna teach you to read, or what?"

We spent the rest of the afternoon and early evening listening to music on the radio as Melody sat and read the story about the big green man who had to hide the fact that he was different from everybody else. Each page was a maze of colourful pictures and adventure. The words were written in boxes and bubbles scattered about the pages. There weren't too many words, and Melody would run her finger beneath them. Sometimes, as she was reading, I would look up at her, and I would feel my heart race. I loved being with her and I would have been happy to stay on that tiny stretch of beach with Melody for the rest of my life. A couple of times she caught me staring and would say, "Isidor, you've got to concentrate! Look at the words and the letters. Listen to the way the letters make words."

So, as those cold days and afternoons turned warmer, and the branches on the trees in the woods exploded with shades of pink blossom, Melody taught me how to read. It wasn't long before I was beginning to understand the letters which made up the words, which then told the story. It helped having the pictures, as when I got stuck, I could look down at the drawings and it all kind of made sense. Then, one bright afternoon, as the tide of the lake lapped about our toes, Melody took a book from the pouch on the front of her apron and handed it to me.

"Isidor, I'm tired of reading – I think you should read me a story now."

I stared down at the book. I felt scared and my stomach knotted. Melody must have seen the fright in my eyes.

Placing a hand over mine, she looked at me and whispered, "There's nothing to fear, Isidor. Books are like doorways. Open it and you can step right into a whole new world."

Running my thumb under the words printed on the cover – the doorway – I read the words aloud. "Grimm's Fairy Stories."

"Now open it," she whispered as if casting a magic spell.

I turned back the cover and tracing the words with my forefinger, just like Melody had taught me, I said, "Rapunzel." I glanced at Melody.

"Carry on," she smiled.

So I did, and I didn't stop until I'd finished. Hour after hour, day after day, Melody would sit beside me on the shore, the radio playing in the background, while she smoked and experimented with the makeup she was slipping into her apron, stolen from the shops. My mother had returned from her trip deep within The Hollows some time ago, and Melody still had to go to school. But I would still sneak away from home, telling my mother I was hanging out with friends, and Melody would come to the lake after school and every weekend. Sometimes she wouldn't show up at all, and I would really miss her.

During the hours that I spent alone down by the lake, I would read the books that Melody had *borrowed* from the library. Then, one spring afternoon as the sun sparkled across the lake, I started to write my first story. It was slow going, but once I had decided to write about the things I had seen and learnt about the humans, my pencil was flying across the scraps of paper I had brought with me from below ground. I didn't share these stories with anyone, not even Melody.

As I sat stooped over my notes, lost in my own little world, I caught sight of someone coming down the shore towards me. I glanced up to see that it was Melody, but something wasn't quite right. She was limping. She dragged her rucksack on the ground beside her with one hand, and in the other I could see she was holding a piece of white paper. I stuffed my notes into my trouser pocket and trotted over to join her.

"Give me that," I said, taking the bag from her. "What's that?" I asked, nodding at the piece of paper.

"A copy of the school dress code," she replied, screwing it up and tossing it away.

"What's happened?"

"A good whipping, that's what happened," she grunted and shuffled forward.

Helping her down onto the sand, she winced in pain. "It's the back of my legs, cut to ribbons they are."

"Your mum whipped you, didn't she?" I glared, feeling a well of anger swell up inside of me.

Melody nodded.

"How do you feel?" and straight away, I regretted asking such a stupid question.

"Awful," she replied through clenched teeth.

"Why did she do it?" I asked, sitting beside her.

"A teacher noticed that I was wearing nail varnish," she explained. "I forgot that I was wearing it. You're not allowed to wear it at school. It's not a big deal, really, but they called my mum. She came up to the school and took me home. She said the usual crap about how the devil was tempting me – and that only whores wear makeup."

"Where is she now?" I snapped, and I couldn't ever remember feeling so angry before. I felt as if I was changing inside somehow, just like Bruce Banner from the comic books that Melody had read to me. My teeth began to ache inside my gums, my fingers started to throb and I clenched my fists. The scars running down the lengths of my arms started to burn and I could feel those little black claws forcing their way out beneath my arms. But there was something else; I could smell blood, the blood which was seeping from the cuts on the backs of Melody's legs. Even though they were hidden from view by her dress, I wanted to taste that blood that dripped from them.

"Where's your mother now?" I asked again, my voice almost a growl.

"She's praying for me," Melody said. Her brow was creased and she added, "Isidor, are you all right?"

"No," I said, taking a step away from her, one hand over my nose to block out the smell of her blood. "I've got to go."

"Go where?" she asked, looking hurt. "I need you."

"Sorry," I almost gagged, then turned and fled.

"Isidor!" Melody called after me.

But I didn't stop. I raced up the shore and into the woods, my heart thumping in my ears. I needed to get back beneath ground – it was like The Hollows were calling to me. But there was another part of me that wanted to stay – that wanted blood and I knew whose blood I needed. Melody's mother's blood. I wanted to rip her fucking heart out and eat it for what she had done to Melody. As I ran, my claws shot from my fingertips. Using them like a set of razorblades, I sliced my coat into a series of ribbons that flew away behind me. I threw my arms open wide on either side of me and released my wings. Then, throwing myself forward, I yanked back the grate that covered the hole and dived inside. I tumbled down the tunnel. Over and over I went, my wings brushing the walls. I hit the bottom. Slamming my fists into the ground, I screamed into the darkness.

Chapter Sixteen

Isidor

I didn't return above ground for a few days. I was sick. In my bed, deep within the Ageless Hill, my body felt as if it were on fire. My mother sat beside me, not once did she leave my side, soaking the sweat from my body with a wet towel. I hungered for the blood that had smelt so sweet as it had ran from Melody's cuts. I had never felt the need for blood before. I had heard rumours that Vampyrus could only stay for so long above ground before the cravings became too much and they had to return to The Hollows. Would the pains that set my soul on fire ever ease? Would they ever go, so I could return above ground? I had to go back. I had to see Melody again.

On the third day, my fever broke and those gut-wrenching pains eased and finally disappeared. I opened my eyes to find my mother sitting beside me, a shawl about her shoulders. She looked tired and drawn.

Seeing my eyes open, she got up from her chair and came to kneel beside me. "Isidor," she whispered and kissed me softly on my brow. "You went above ground, didn't you?"

"Yes," I said, my throat feeling sore.

"Why?" she asked, but she didn't sound angry, just scared. What frightened her so much, I didn't understand at that time. I didn't know then, that she was my aunt and not my mother. I think she must have feared I would find out the truth somehow.

"I just had to see it for myself," I croaked, and she handed me a cup of water. I sipped at it until the pain in my throat eased.

"Promise me you won't go back," she said, brushing the hair from my forehead.

"I can't promise that, mother," I said, handing her the cup.

"Why not?" and I could see tears standing in her eyes. It

was like she believed that she would lose me – like I might never come back again.

"I just have to see someone," I said. "I just have to see my friend."

"Who?"

"A girl," I said. "I can't just leave her. She has helped me so much."

"Helped you with what?" Mother asked me.

"With everything," I told her, and swung my legs over the edge of the bed. It was freezing cold, and I shivered.

"You're still ill, Isidor," she said, trying to throw a blanket around my shoulders.

"I'm fine," I tried to convince her.

"Wait just a few more days, then go," she said, and I read the fear in her eyes.

"What are you so scared of?" I asked softy.

"You're different to them," she said, and gently stroked my face.

"We're all different, and that's good, isn't it?" I said, pulling on my clothes.

I stood in the alcove and looked back at her. "I love you, mum," I smiled.

"Isidor, don't fall in love with a human," she warned me. "It will only lead to heartache."

"How do you figure that?" I asked her.

"Because we are not like them and they are not like us," she said. "You will have to lead a life of lies and deceit. You could never tell her what you truly are. It is forbidden for the Vampyrus and humans to breed. If you don't love yourself, Isidor, then love this girl enough not to deceive her. Come back to The Hollows before you cause her any hurt."

With my mother's warning ringing in my ears, I went back above ground.

I headed through the woods and down towards the lake in search of Melody. It had been four days since I had last seen her. Had she believed that I had gone for good – never to come back? I had to see her, explain if I could, why I had fled that day, and left her when she had needed me most.

With the wind pulling at my hair and clothes, I raced down to the shore, but I couldn't see Melody. I headed for the bush where we had spent so many days together. In the middle sat the ashes of the burnt out fire she had lit to keep us warm. She wasn't there, either. The only other place that I could think of finding her was home.

So, it was with some trepidation that I approached Melody's house and knocked on the door. I hadn't seen her mum since I had hidden in the wardrobe. I knocked on the door. After several moments of waiting patiently, the door swung slowly ajar and Melody's mum peered at me through the gap she had created. Her face looked older than I pictured it to be. She had deep lines around her nose and mouth. Her hair was darkish grey and her lips looked taught and puckered.

"Hello," I said. "My name is Isidor Smith."

"What do you want?" she asked suspiciously.

"I was hoping I could speak with your daughter."

"Daughter? What Daughter?" she said. "I haven't got a daughter."

"Yeah, you do," I said confused. "Melody."

"Nope, sorry, you're mistaken. Never had no daughter – never had any children," she insisted.

I wondered if she was madder than I first thought, or had she completely cut Melody out of her life and memory because of what she had done? Could her mother be that ashamed of her?

"Please can I see her?" I asked, feeling desperate now.

"Are you mad?" she croaked.

No, but you are - I was tempted to say, but bit my tongue.

"*Go away!*" she cursed as she went to shut the door in my face.

I planted my foot between the door and the frame, forcing it open.

"Get your foot out of my door before I call the cops!" she threatened.

"You do have a daughter and her name is Melody..." I started.

"Yakadee - Yakadee - Yak!" she cackled. "I ain't listening because I never had no daughter! Now get off my porch!"

I realised I was wasting my time and probably stirring up more trouble for Melody. So I withdrew my foot from her door, which she instantly closed in my face. I stepped away and moved towards the steps leading from her porch and then suddenly, I turned back and shouted at the closed door, "You say you're a *religious* woman! Well if you are - *pray* for your own soul, because you're gonna need all the prayers that you can get, you old witch."

I then stepped off her porch and walked away. I hadn't gone far, when I looked back at the house, and there looking back at me from the upstairs front window was Melody. Standing in the lane that cut through the fields to her house, I raised my hand in the air and waved. I couldn't help the stupid grin that cut across my face. I was so happy to see her again. Instead of waving, Melody pressed the flat of her hand to the windowpane and hung her head.

Then, not caring who saw me, or how different I was to anyone else, I slowly removed my coat. It dropped to the ground, and then raising my arms, I looked up at the window to see Melody staring down at me once more, her hand still pressed against the window as if reaching out for me. Without taking my eyes from hers, I opened my arms and let my wings unfold. As they did, I could feel my feet lifting from the ground. With the wind snagging at my hair, I glided up to her window. I hovered outside as she stared back at me. She was either gonna freak out and run away, or she was...

Melody pushed open the window. "Isidor, are you an angel?" she asked me softly.

"I don't come from heaven, if that's what you mean," I smiled.

"Where do you come from?" she whispered, still not taking her eyes from mine.

"Below ground," I told her.

"So you're a dead angel?" she whispered over the sound of the wind that blew about the eaves.

Reaching through the open window, I took her hand and

placed it against my chest so she could feel my racing heart. "Do I feel dead?" I asked her.

"No," she breathed. "Why is your heart beating so fast?"

I didn't want to tell her the reason – I couldn't. So instead, I lifted her into my arms and said, "Let's be us – just for one day."

Then, rolling my shoulders back, I soared up into the sky with her wrapped in my arms. I carried her up into the clouds and it was freedom. I soared high, and Melody clung to me. We spiralled over the fields, hills, and mountains. The feeling of not having to hide my wings or who or what I really was felt incredible. To share that moment with Melody was wonderful.

We swooped out of the sky and gently landed on the shore by the lake. With Melody still in my arms, I untied the strings that held her bonnet in place and removed it. And just like the girl, Rapunzel, her hair fell free, spilling over her shoulders and down her back in thick coils. It was the first time I had seen her hair free and I gasped as it shone in the fading sunlight.

"Don't you like it?" she asked me nervously.

"It's beautiful," I told her, losing my hands deep within its curls. It felt like silk running over my fingers.

Then gently, she ran the tips of her fingers across my wings, and down the length of my scars. "That's why you fled that day, wasn't it?" she said mesmerised.

"Yes," I told her. "I could feel myself changing and I thought you would be scared of me."

"I always wondered what these scars were," she said thoughtfully.

"Why didn't you ask?"

"It was your secret and I knew that you would tell me one day – when you were ready," she said.

"You're not scared of me?" I asked her, my heart still racing.

"How could I be scared of an angel?" she whispered, looking up at me. "Angels help people, don't they? They watch over you and make sure you are safe. I always knew that you were different from the others, and now I know why."

"Thank you," I smiled, our faces so close now that the tips of our noses were almost touching. I wanted to kiss her, but didn't know if I should.

"Thank you for what?" she breathed, and her breath felt warm against my cheek.

"For liking me for who I am. For not wanting to put me in a cage and open me up to see how I work. For not laughing at me because I couldn't read and write," I told her.

"Thank you for not being cruel to me for how I dress and the way I live. Thank you for taking the loneliness away. I was so tired of being lonely, Isidor."

Hearing her say this broke my heart as I knew that I couldn't stay. I would have to go back to The Hollows. I couldn't forget my mother's warning, and I didn't want to hurt Melody by staying because we could never be together. Neither could I live with being tempted by the need for human blood. If I went, my cravings would certainly go, but her loneliness would return. Not having the courage to tell her just yet, I took her hands in mine and said, "I've got something for you."

"What?" she asked, her eyes brightening.

I led Melody up the shore to our makeshift camp in the bushes. Once inside, we sat down. As I reached into my pocket, Melody rummaged around in the undergrowth and pulled a stale pack of cigarettes from beneath some moss. She lit one. From my pocket, I took the notes that I had been writing on.

"What's that?" she asked me.

"It's not very good," I said.

"What is it?"

"It's a story I've written," I explained. "I'm going to write more. I'm going to call them *Isidor's Penny Dreadfuls*."

"Why call them that?" she asked, looking confused.

"Because they'll be so dreadful that people probably wouldn't even pay a penny for them," I half-laughed.

"What's it about?" she asked, eagerly moving closer towards me.

"It's a story about the things I've seen and learnt about above ground," I explained. "I wrote it for you."

With a smile on her lips and eyes bright, she said, "Isidor, I want to hear you read one of your own stories."

"Are you sure?" I asked her.

"Just read, Isidor, that's what you always wanted to do, isn't it?"

So, with Melody resting her head against my shoulder, and my first Penny Dreadful in my hand, this is the story that I read to her.

Chapter Seventeen

'A Special Friend'
By
Isidor Smith

Michael Blake swung his legs over the side of the bed and fixed his thin, fragile feet firmly to the wooden floor. The boards which lined the floor of his poky bedroom were rough and he had lost count of how many times he had picked splinters from the balls of his feet. The sheets lay grey and unwashed at the foot of his bed.

Michael sat hunched forward, and warmed his bare shoulders by rubbing them vigorously with his hands. He raised his pale and gaunt face and peered about the dimly-lit room. His grey eyes were ringed with dark, sleepless shadows. Michael stood up on two bony legs and gave a long tired yawn. He arched his back and stretched out his arms, hoping the tiredness would leave him. As he did this, his skimpy vest rose upwards, showing off a set of ribs, which stuck through his skin like rungs on a ladder. He was way too thin for fourteen. Michael let his body relax and the vest dropped back into place, covering his emaciated body once again. He preferred it like that. He crossed the room and pulled back the curtains and looked out at the new day.

It was still dark outside and lights glimmered in the bedroom and kitchen windows from the house across the street. A milk float could be heard as it turned into the street. It rattled, jangled, and hummed as it came. The milk float stopped. Michael watched the driver get out, collect a crate of milk, and deliver bottles to the house across the street. Michael knew that he wouldn't be getting any milk today as his father hadn't been able to pay the bill. Michael let go of the curtain and it swung back into place. He turned and dressed for school.

Michael switched on the light and the bare bulb was hardly powerful enough to light the room. His bedroom was bare. The only furniture he had was his bed and a chair on which he hung his clothes. Beside his bed sat a small table and on this was an old fashioned looking alarm clock. He screwed up his eyes and peered at the hands on it. They read half past seven. The alarm clock might have been old, but it was never wrong. The walls inside his room were also bare, apart from his friend, that is.

Michael's friend was Marilyn Monroe. The poster of her hung alone on his wall. She wasn't like an everyday friend. Marilyn had been dead fifty years and had died thirty-six years before he had been born. But the picture of her was special to him. It was company for Michael and he needed that badly. He had no mother and a father who was interested in climbing into a bottle of Jack Daniels instead of spending time with him. Michael didn't have any friends, either. He was the school scapegoat. Every school had one. So Michael took comfort by believing that Marilyn was his friend. Just his. But of course she wasn't. Marilyn was dead. Michael didn't trouble himself with such thoughts because he knew that they were special friends. He knew he wasn't mad, he knew he didn't imagine the conversations he had with her. At first Michael thought he was losing the plot, but after she had changed position in the poster on the wall and had joked, "It's so tiring standing in the same pose," he was sure it was for real. But if Michael were to be honest with himself, he did have doubts. But he had no one to confide in and even if he had, would they have believed him? Would you?

Michael tightened his school tie about his neck, put on his trousers, socks, and navy-blue sweater. He bent over the pile of school books on his bedroom floor and sorted through them. The school timetable buzzed around inside his head as he tried hard to remember the lessons he had for that day. But being so tired and weak feeling, it was hard for him to remember. Once he was sure he had collected the books he needed, he stuffed them under his arm. He straightened his messy black hair with his fingers. He looked up at the glossy poster of Marilyn, her head tilted to one side, thick red lips smiling down at him. She was wearing a one-piece swimsuit. One of her legs was slightly bent at the knee, both hands rested against her thighs. He thought she looked beautiful in that particular pose.

Michael took a step closer to the poster, and with a smile, he whispered, "See you later, Marilyn."

He turned for the door, and as he did, he was sure that he heard...heard what? Maybe it was just the wind blowing outside. Michael jerked his head back towards the poster. Marilyn stood just as she had only moments before. Had she spoken to him? He couldn't be sure.

Am I really going mad? He wondered to himself.

Am I really that lonely – that desperate for a friend of my own that I'm imagining that I am hearing the voice of a movie star long dead?

Confused, Michael shook his head and set off for school.

Michael hurried down the street, his coat fastened up to his neck, stooped forward to protect himself against the bitter wind. Tree branches moved gracefully back and forth in the early autumn storm like the arms of ballerinas. Leaves whisked along the gutter, getting caught in the storm drains. Silver drops of rain started to fall and they almost seemed to dance in the glare of the streetlights. Cars drove slowly past, the tyres hissing against the wet road, the windscreen wipers squeaking.

Michael hurried on, clutching school books to his chest, protecting them from the rain. He tugged on his hood, which swung behind him. The school building loomed ahead and I hated the sight of it. Other children hurried past towards the school, eager to get there. Michael dashed across the puddled schoolyard and towards the bike sheds. Other boys took shelter in there. Some were talking, sharing jokes, and laughing. Others hid in the corners and secretly smoked. Michael found himself a quiet corner. Some of the other kids turned their heads and stared at him. Others made remarks loud enough for him to overhear.

"Hey, Ribs!" one of them shouted and the others laughed.

Ribs had been his nickname for as long as he could remember.

A tall boy who looked more like a man than a school kid

shouted, "It's time you beefed yourself up, Blake."

Another hollered, "Be careful of the wind, Blake, you might just blow away!"

The crowd in the bike shed laughed and cheered the others on. There was a sense of cruel excitement building. The boy who looked almost a man, his name was Steve Edwards, came forward. He leaned into Michael's face and said, "Why are you so fucking weird?"

More laughter from the crowd.

Michael stood silently and made no reply. He held onto his books like a drowning man might cling to an inflatable. Edwards loomed over Michael and the crowd fell silent. Then, taking his huge club-like hands from his pockets, he shoved Michael hard in the chest, sending his books spilling from his arms. Again, Michael refused to look up at his tormentor. Instead he crouched down and started to gather them up. Seeing this, Edwards kicked them away, out of reach.

"Why are you so fucking weird?" Edwards said. "No one gives a shit about school books."

"Because you probably can't read them," Michael said under his breath. But he didn't say it quietly enough.

"Say what?" Edwards said, looking back over his shoulder at his friends and winking slyly at them.

"Nothing," Michael whispered.

"What did you say?" Edwards pushed him in the chest again, sending Michael staggering backwards.

Michael stayed silent – hoping Edwards would soon get bored and go away. He had bullied Michael ever since the first grade.

"How is that pissed-up old man of yours?" Edwards teased and the crowd sniggered. "I heard he lost his job."

Michael said nothing.

"You're so much like him," Edwards came again. "Nothing but a freaking loser. No wonder your mother fucked off with that other guy."

"My mother died of cancer," Michael said.

"Whatever," Edwards spat. "We all know that's the bullshit excuse your father put around town because he was too embarrassed to admit that his wife was being slipped a length by some other guy."

Michael clenched his fists by his sides and stayed looking at the ground.

"So if your mum really is dead, why hasn't your dad got himself another bit of skirt?" Edwards sneered. "Maybe it's because he's like you and couldn't get laid in a whorehouse?"

This time, Michael did raise his head and looked at Edwards with his sunken eyes.

"God, you're so freaking creepy," Edwards said. "No wonder you don't have any friends, standing there like some freaking skeleton."

"I do have a friend," Michael said, staring hard into Edwards's eyes.

"Do you?" Edwards mocked, looking all around him. "I don't see him."

"My friend's not a he – they're a she," Michael said, brushing past Edwards in an attempt to get away. He knew that he had said enough already.

Edwards stuck his hand into Michael's chest and pinned him back into the corner of the shed. The crowd fell silent. "Are you taking the piss?" he asked, leaning into Michael. "Is she by any chance imaginary?"

"No!" Michael snapped.

Why shouldn't I tell him? Why shouldn't I tell all of them about my friend? He thought to himself. But he knew why.

"What's her name?" Edwards sneered, but there was something in his voice that suggested that he wasn't sure if Michael was telling the truth or not.

"Marilyn Mon..." The words had slipped from Michael's mouth before he had even realised what he had said. Then he was gone, shoving his way past Edwards and racing away across the schoolyard. As he fled, he heard someone shout from the crowd "Roe!" and they all fell about laughing.

But Edwards stared after Michael and he thought he had seen something in those eyes – it was like he had been telling the truth somehow. Pushing those thoughts from his head, Edwards sneered to himself and said "Marilyn Monroe, what a load of old *bollocks!"*

Michael ran through the pouring rain and didn't stop until he got home. He would skip school today. It wasn't as if his father would even notice. As he ran, rain washed away the tears that streaked down his cheeks. He pushed against the front door and slipped inside. At the foot of the stairs, he glanced into the living room to see his father lying unconscious on the sofa, congealed vomit down the front of his vest. Michael headed up the stairs. Entering his room, he closed the door behind him. He was never seen again.

There was a police investigation into Michael's disappearance, but he was never found. It was eventually believed he had run away to London, lost amongst the other thousands of homeless people there. Michael's room was searched, but all they found was his filthy clothes, tattered school books, and a torn up poster of Marilyn Monroe.

Nobody had seen or heard from Michael since his disappearance – until today.

Steve Edwards picked up the postcard off the doormat and carried it up to his bedroom. Sitting on the edge of his blue quilted bed, he looked at it. There wasn't a message written on the back, just his name and address, which looked slightly smudged. When he turned the postcard over in his hands, he knew who had sent it and his blood froze.

It was a postcard of Marilyn Monroe standing over a subway grating from the movie 'The Seven Year Itch' which had been made in 1955. Her white flowing dress was flowing up around her thighs as she stood in front of several hundred screaming fans.

Steve looked at the postcard and felt ill. Standing amongst the adoring fans, contented and happy-looking at last, was Michael.

Chapter Eighteen

Isidor

I took my notes, folded them in half, and put them back in my trouser pocket. Melody didn't say anything and I guessed she hated it – that she thought it was a stupid story.

Unable to bear the silence any longer, I peeked at her and said, "It was dreadful, wasn't it?"

Holding out her hand, she said, "Give me your notes."

I took them from my pocket, as the leaves surrounding our camp rustled in the wind. Not knowing why she wanted them, I handed her the crinkled scraps of paper.

Melody took them, and placing them into the pocket of her apron, she looked at me and said, "Isidor, that was wonderful."

"Get out of here," I said, feeling embarrassed, "You're just saying that."

"The ending was magical," she said. "Just imagine if you could go someplace else – to a place where you could be happy. That would be magical, right?"

"I guess," I said thoughtfully.

"You know it would be magical or you wouldn't have written that story," she said. Melody sat quietly for a moment, then added, "I was Michael, wasn't I?"

"Yes," I said, slowly nodding my head.

"The only difference is that I don't have anyone to take me someplace else," she whispered.

To hear her say this made me want to take her back to The Hollows with me, but could I? Would she really want to live beneath ground for the rest of her life? What would the Vampyrus think? We were meant to live in secret. Humans weren't meant to know about us. I'd also heard the stories about the Vampyrus who were unable to fight their cravings for human blood. It could be dangerous for her. Pushing away the thoughts of taking her home with me, I changed the subject and said, "Can I ask you something?"

"Sure," she said.

"Some days you don't show up at the lake at all. Where do you go and what do you do?" I asked her.

"It doesn't matter," she said, looking away.

"Why won't you tell me?" I pushed gently.

"You know you said that just for today, we should be us," she reminded me.

"Yes," I smiled.

"Today I can't be me," Melody said, and pulled the hem of her dress down. "But one day soon."

"Why not today?"

But before she had a chance to answer me, there was a noise from just outside our camp. Looking at each other, we got up and made our way out. With my wings hidden again, I clambered from the bushes and stumbled straight into the path of Ray Baines. Barry, the bucktooth donkey and Lucy were with him.

"For God's sake," I moaned to myself, hoping that I would never have had to see Ray and his friends again.

"You got me in the shit good and proper the other day with that cop!" Ray scowled at me, and gone was the scared-looking kid I had seen cowering in front of his father. "It was you who stole that book, and you weren't even man enough to own up to it."

"You shouldn't have stolen my coat," I said back.

Donkey-boy sniggered and Ray glared at him. Lucy was staring at my arms again. What freaks.

Then, Melody stumbled from the bushes behind me.

"Whoa! Who have we got here?" Ray said upon seeing Melody.

"They've been getting it on in the bushes!" donkey-boy screeched excitedly.

"With her?" Lucy said in disbelief. "But she's, like, some kinda nun or something."

"It's the quiet ones you have to watch," Ray said, reaching forward, trying to lift up the hem of Melody's dress. Melody slapped his hand away. "I just want to see your titties."

"Fuck off!" Melody hissed.

"Whoo-hoo!" donkey-boy laughed and clapped his hands feverishly together. "The nun swears!"

"What will your freak mother say about that?" Lucy asked.

I positioned myself in front of Melody. "Why don't you three just go away?" I said, trying to stay calm.

"Why should you get all the fun?" Ray glared at me. "How about the nun gives me and my friend Barry over here a hand job each and we won't tell her mum what she's been up to in the bushes with you."

"That's not going to happen," I said, staring back at him.

"What? She's not going to give us a hand job, or we're not going to tell her mum that she's been screwing you?" Ray said, taking a step closer towards me.

"Neither is gonna happen," I told him as I stood in front of Melody.

"And you're gonna stop me, I guess?" Ray said, raising his fists.

I had no intention of fighting Ray. So I stepped forward and said, "What are you gonna do, Ray, whoop my arse? Beat me? *Shoot* me with one of your dad's big fuck-off guns? Then what are ya gonna do? Get Melody to whack you off? Then what? Beat her, too?" I taunted him.

He narrowed the gap even more, shoving his shirtsleeves up his forearms.

Melody tugged at my arm and whispered, "C'mon, Isidor, let's just get outer here."

"What, and spend the rest of our lives running from *bullies* like him?" I said, staring into Ray's eyes.

"You should listen to your girlfriend and run while you still can," Ray threatened.

Even though my heart was slamming against my chest plate, I stood my ground. "Do what you have to do then. Beat me, kill me! But I promise you, even if I have to crawl on my hands and fucking knees, I'm gonna tell every last motherfucker in this town that really, you're just a scared little boy." I looked in the direction of donkey-boy and Lucy, who were standing just a few feet behind Ray. They looked at each other as if not knowing what I was talking about.

Ray looked momentarily shocked by what I had said, and sensing this, I continued. "Would daddy be proud of his son if he knew that he bullied girls, tried to get them to whack him off? I reckon he'll be bursting with so much pride, he'll award you the 'Jerk-off of the year award'!"

As soon as I mentioned Ray's father, he physically flinched backwards away from me. It was then that it finally dawned on me what Ray's true weakness was.

"I get it, I get it! So who's scared of their daddy then?" I taunted him.

"Shut your fucking mouth!" he groaned.

Once I knew his weakness, I said, "So daddy doesn't love you? Is that it?"

"*Shut-up!*" Ray screeched.

"Or is it that daddy loves you *too* much? The bad kinda love that he says is perfectly okay, but just don't tell your momma about it!"

"*Shut-up! Shut-up! Shut-up!*" he wailed, placing his hands over his ears.

I felt awful and spiteful all at the same time, but I knew I had him and this was my chance to lay down a few of my own ground rules before I went back to The Hollows and left Melody above ground on her own.

"I'll shut-up if you promise you'll leave Melody alone, and that goes for donkey-boy and Lucy."

"I promise," he whispered.

"I can't hear you!" I shouted.

"*I promise!*" he cried.

"I think at last we've come to an understanding, and we got there without the use of any violence. A first for you, I suspect," I said dryly. "Now get out of here!"

Ray turned and fled up the shore, donkey-boy and Lucy following him.

"Isidor, you did it," Melody said in amazement. "You've got him off my back."

"I hope so," I replied wistfully. "I'm not sure, though."

"How come?"

"Ray has problems, serious problems with his dad. I just hope I haven't gone and made them a whole lot worse," I said, as I stood and watched him and his friends disappear into the distance.

Melody collected her bonnet from where it lay in the sand. She tucked her hair beneath it and retied the strings. Taking her in my arms, I released my wings and carried her up into the sky. It was getting dark as we raced silently through the clouds together.

We hovered momentarily above her home, then I swooped her down out of the sky. I helped Melody back through her bedroom window.

"When will I see you again?" she asked me. But before I'd the chance to answer, she placed a finger against my lips and said, "Just be at the town swimming pool, in three days' time."

"Why?" I asked with a frown, floating just outside her window.

"There is going to be a swimming tournament," she explained. "It's to celebrate the twenty-fifth anniversary of my school and they are throwing this big swimming gala for the town. I'm doing something special. I doubt I'll be very good."

"So why do you want me to be there?" I asked.

"Just be there," she said and closed the window.

Chapter Nineteen

Isidor

I returned to The Hollows and spent the next three days there. I didn't go out once. I spent the days and most of the nights writing. I couldn't stop. My head was full of so many stories. Some were better than others, but most of them, I guessed, were dreadful. My mother didn't seem too concerned that I spent so much of my time alone. I think she was just pleased I had come home.

At night, as I lay on my bed, I thought of Melody. However much I tried, I just couldn't stop thinking about her. Eyes open or shut, I could see her. The more I thought about her, the more I knew that I couldn't leave her alone above ground. To think of her living with her mother, spending her life imprisoned behind that long dress, apron, and bonnet made me sad. Even if Ray kept his promise and left her alone from now on, there would be others who would be quick to ridicule and hurt her.

Maybe I could bring her to The Hollows? I wondered. Maybe she would be happy here? Would my mother really object, if it meant me staying in The Hollows, instead of staying above ground? I made up my mind that I would tell Melody everything about me and the world that I came from and ask her to come back with me. Once my decision had been made, I felt as if a weight had been taken from me, and I slept easier. But I knew in my heart that I didn't just want Melody to come back to The Hollows so I could save her; the real reason was, I didn't want to be apart from her.

On the third day, I waited for my mother to head off to work in the caves, and I once again snuck above ground. I made my way through the woods and followed the road in to the town of Lake Lure. The town seemed busier than usual, and I found the swimming pool without too much trouble. It was a building that had been decorated with flags, and a car park full of school buses. Keeping my head down, I lost myself amongst the other spectators who had come to see the swimming gala.

Rows of chairs had been placed around the edge of the swimming pool and I took a seat at the back. A raised platform had been erected and this had been put in place for school staff and the town mayor to sit on. I also noticed a guy with a big camera who wore a badge that read: *PRESS*.

As the headmaster stood on the raised platform and welcomed the parents and the mayor, I glanced around the swimming pool and saw Ray and his friends sitting close to the water. They obviously weren't taking part, as they were dressed in their school uniforms. Once the headmaster had finished his speech, the gala began.

It was made up of several races, each winner being presented with a small trophy. In between each race there was swimming performed to music. At the end of each demonstration, the crowd erupted into applause and the classes, which had been represented, cheered for their classmates. The only pupil I hadn't seen was Melody. As the gala came to its end, the headmaster stood and spoke to the school and all the spectators once again.

"I'm sure you'll all agree that this has been a wonderful event today. It goes to illustrate the school's team spirit and love of sports. But ladies and gentlemen, the day is not over yet. We now have something very special for you. We are very proud of this young athlete. I understand she has been working tirelessly for some weeks to put on a spectacular finale. It is with great pleasure that I now introduce, Melody Rose."

Melody appeared from the changing room, and with her head bowed low, she made her way over to the ladder that led to the diving board, which towered above the swimming pool. She was dressed in a white swimming robe that trailed behind her. Her hair was covered with a swimming cap. So was this why she had often gone missing? I wondered. Had Melody secretly been practising a spectacular dive? Why hadn't she mentioned it? Was this why she had asked me to come today – so I could see what it was that she really wanted to do with her life? I scanned the faces of the spectators gathered around the pool, but couldn't see her mother. Maybe she didn't know. Perhaps if her mother had found out, it would have been something else she would have stopped Melody from doing. I could understand why she had kept it a secret.

I watched from the back row as Melody passed the rows of her fellow pupils, teachers, town mayor and the guy from the press. She only looked up once and that was at me. We made eye contact and she winked. It was only then that I sensed something was up, that she had something planned.

I watched Melody climb the ladder to the diving board. As she reached the top, the room fell into silence. I glanced around at the wall of people, and all of them had their heads tilted back on their necks, as they looked up at my friend, my best friend.

Melody stood on the end of the diving board, motionless. She seemed to stand there forever. Then without warning, she pulled off the robe and the swimming cap that she was wearing. There was an audible gasp from the crowd as they stared up in complete shock. Even I let out the faintest of gasps, and sat with mouth open, my jaw almost touching my chest, as I stared up at Melody.

She stood tall and proud, her back as straight as a ruler, her arms swinging by her hips. Around the pool, it was perfectly still and silent. I blinked in complete surprise and shock, and then an uncontrollable smile spread across my face.

Oh, Melody, I thought to myself as I looked at her standing up there naked, her hair now bright pink. But in a way, she didn't look naked – not really. She was covered in so many tattoos that she looked as if she were wearing a brightly decorated body stocking. The roses started at her ankles and spread across her entire body. Each tattooed rose was attached to a vine, which snaked its way from her feet, up her legs, over her thighs, across her buttocks, the flat of her tummy, back, breasts, and neck.

So that's where she disappeared to, I smiled to myself.

But there was one rose which was brighter than the rest, and it had been tattooed over her heart. It was then I realised all of the other roses, apart from this one, were closed.

The one over her left breast was open, and shards of bright white light had been tattooed streaming from it. To look at that open rose, I knew that Melody was flowering, too.

Then, as I watched her, she looked down at me and shouted, "For one day, Isidor, I just want to be me."

Melody then tumbled over and over through the air, as if in slow motion. Her descent seemed to last an eternity. The entire audience had their eyes transfixed on Melody as she flipped, rotated, and spun towards the pool. She hit the water with an almighty *'splosh!'* and disappeared from view. As if by magic, the sound of her hitting the water tore the rest of us from our trance.

Melody popped her head up from beneath the water, and immediately looked at me with the biggest smile I had ever seen spread across anyone's face. With that, every pupil in attendance jumped out of their seats and the sounds of their cheers was deafening.

Seeing this, Melody dove back under the water, kicking her legs in the air as she disappeared like an exotic mermaid. She resurfaced within moments and started punching the air with her fist. The other pupils just went berserk. They were whistling, cheering, screaming, and slapping each other on the back. I looked all around me, and to my surprise and secret delight, I spotted Ray in the crowd, and even he was up on his feet cheering and punching the air with his fist. The atmosphere was electric. It was as if Melody had triggered something in all of them. Any resentment or frustration, pent-up dislike for the school, their parents, or society seemed to explode from within all of them. To watch the humans like this was the most exhilarating feeling I had ever had.

I looked back at Melody again as she swam back and forth, occasionally stopping to wave at the crowd. She was rolling her head back and laughing and I don't think I had ever seen her so happy. She looked at me again and made a circle with her thumb and forefinger. I was so proud of her, that I thought my heart was going to burst from my chest.

It was then that I looked towards the stage where the staff and mayor were seated, and they were obviously not sharing in the pupils' delight. Most of the teachers looked as if they were just about to have heart attacks and the Mayor looked as if someone had just shown him conclusive proof that he had been secretly sleeping with whores for the last twenty years! The press guy was having a great time as he was busily snapping away.

The headmaster was on his feet and his head looked like a swollen tomato as he gestured furiously at the swimming pool and barked orders at some of the teachers. One of the teachers dived into the water, without removing his jacket, shooting beneath the water towards Melody.

Melody was now backstroking her way around the pool in a lap of honour, basking in her newfound glory. I tried to shout a warning to her, but my cries were drowned out by the bedlam that surrounded me. The teacher circled her like a shark, then darted towards Melody with lightning speed and dragged her under the water. Seeing this, the crowd began to turn hostile. The school kids started to boo and heckle as the teacher wrestled Melody out of the water.

With the help of two other teachers who were waiting by the edge of the pool, they dragged Melody towards the changing room door. Even though Melody continued to squirm in their arms, she still managed to find me in the crowd and smile. I smiled back. Then, she was gone, hurried away into the changing rooms and out of view.

As the headmaster tried to restore some order to the proceedings, I snuck from the hall and headed for the lake.

Chapter Twenty

Isidor

Desperate to see Melody again, I waited for her. I wanted to know that she was okay. I prayed that her mum hadn't made her suffer for what she had done at school. When Melody arrived, I would tell her that she didn't have to return home, that she could come to The Hollows with me. I waited at the bush for hours, and just when I thought she would never show, I saw a figure heading along the shore towards me. With my heart leaping in my chest, I raced towards her. But as I drew closer, I knew it wasn't her. It was Ray, and I prepared myself for some childish taunts.

"Isidor, I need to speak to you!" he shouted, hurrying towards me.

"I'm not in the mood, Ray. Have you forgotten our agreement?" I hissed at him.

"It's about Melody. I've got some news about Melody," he persisted.

I stopped in my tracks, turned, and eyed him suspiciously. "This better not be the build-up to some kinda sick joke, because if it is…"

"No, no, it's not, I promise," he pushed, sounding out of breath.

"Okay," I said. "What do you know?"

"Melody's mum is sending her away!"

"Sending her where?"

"Dunno. I just know that after that incident at the pool, her mum has decided to send her away."

"How do you know all this," I quizzed, still suspicious that what he was telling me was a lie.

"My mum goes to the same prayer group as Melody's mum. Apparently, they've all been talking and praying about it. They say she's evil and must be sent way!"

My stomach somersaulted at hearing this and I began to

panic. "When's she going? Do you know when?" I pleaded.

"Right now," Ray gasped, still drawing breath.

I turned on my heels and began to set off, then looking back at Ray I said, "Why would you help me like this? You hate me and Melody."

"I've kinda been thinking a lot lately, especially since Melody did her thing at the pool today. She ain't all bad, I guess. I was hoping we could put all that other stuff behind us - if you wanted to, that is?"

"You surprise me, Ray," I said, genuinely shocked. "I thought you were a dumbass, but maybe I was wrong about you, too. Thanks for your help. I owe you one."

"No, you don't. I think that makes us even. Now get out of here, before you miss your friend."

I ran as fast as I could to Melody's house.

I turned into the road that led to her home and nearly got mowed down by Melody's mother as she sped towards me in her car. I pressed myself against the bushes, and as she passed, I caught a glimpse of Melody sitting motionlessly in the backseat. Her face was grey and I could see that her long, pink hair had all been shaved off. Melody had no hair left; she looked like a prisoner of war. The car slowed as it neared the bottom of the track and I ran alongside it, banging on the window to get Melody's attention.

"Melody! It's me, Melody!" I shouted.

She looked at me through the window and her face was expressionless. I banged again with my fist against the side of the car.

"Melody! Melody!"

The car reached the end of the track, then sped up as it turned onto the main road. I knew that I could keep up with the car; If I released my wings, but I couldn't risk being seen. The humans didn't like *different*, my mother had told me that. With all the air that I had left in my lungs, I shouted one last time at the disappearing car.

"Melody!"

I saw the taillights glow an angry red as the car slowed

at the stop-lights up ahead. I thought about chasing after it again, but I knew in my heart that by the time I had drawn level with it, the lights would have changed to 'GO' and the car would be gone again. Then suddenly, I saw the back door fly open and Melody jumped out. She started to run as fast as she could towards me. I raced forwards like a runner flying out of the starting-blocks. I ran as fast as I could towards her, down the centre of the road. I was aware of the sound of cars breaking hard and the wailing sounds of car horns as drivers honked at me.

"Get out of the road!" someone shouted.

I blocked these sounds out and ran towards my friend. We reached each other and Melody fell into my arms.

"She's sending me away, Isidor. She's sending me away!" Melody panted.

"Where's she sending you?" I asked desperately.

"I don't know," she said and I could see the fear in her eyes.

"When will you be back?"

"I don't think I ever will. She's sending me away for good!"

"Come with -" I started, but Melody was being yanked away from me.

"Keep away from her!" Melody's mum yelled, pulling at her.

"Let her stay," I begged.

"It's because of wicked boys like you that I'm sending her away!" she seethed.

She began to wrestle with Melody as she pulled her back towards the car, which was now completely blocking the road with a queue of cars behind it, all blasting their horns. Melody managed to break free from her mum and came running back towards me again. She threw her arms around me and whispered in my ear.

"I love you, Isidor. Thank you for being my friend."

"I love you too, Melody. Please don't go!" I said, beginning to feel the burning sensation of tears on my cheeks. "Stay. I'll miss you...come with me..."

Her mum was on us again. This time she was trying to wedge herself between us and prise us apart.

"Leave my daughter alone, you evil boy!" she seethed.

"But she's my friend..." I tried to reason with her through my tears.

"She doesn't need a friend like you!" she screamed, pulling at the both of us.

I looked at Melody and her eyes were red and streaming with tears.

"I'm so glad I got to meet you, Melody" I cried as I let go of her hand.

The sleeve of her dress rode up her arm and I could see purple coloured rope burns eating into her wrists. It was then I realised I had to let her go. Wherever her mum was sending Melody, it had to be better than being stuck with her.

I watched without moving, as she dragged Melody back to her car, bundling her onto the backseat. I stood and cried as I watched Melody peering at me through the rear window. I didn't move from that spot until she disappeared into the distance and out of my life. It was then, as I stood alone, I realised there was something wrapped around my fingers. I looked down and saw Melody's rosary beads swinging from my hand. Unwinding them, I placed them around my neck and have never taken them off.

Chapter Twenty-One

Isidor

I didn't care if I never came above ground again. I hated it. But before I left, there were two things I knew I had to do, and one of those was to say thank-you to Ray. He wasn't my friend, but if it hadn't have been for him, I wouldn't have gotten the chance to say goodbye to Melody.

Wiping the tears from my eyes, I set off in the direction of his house. It was almost nightfall by the time I reached it. There was a light on downstairs, in the room that I'd seen Ray and his father in before. I only got halfway up the front path when I heard his father's raised voice again. Just like I had before, I crouched down and crept through the neatly kept flowerbeds, until I was positioned beneath the window.

From my hiding place, I heard Ray's father say, "I'm going to make a man of you, Raymond. You need to muscle up and grow up. I'm going to teach you some exercises that will put some meat on those bones of yours."

"But I don't want to..." Ray started.

"Don't you dare disobey me," I heard his father bark. "It's about time you became a man instead of messing about with your friends. You'll be in the army soon."

"I don't want..."

"*Quiet!*" he roared and his voice was so loud and angry sounding that I flinched beneath the window. "Now get undressed."

Very carefully, I eased myself up and peered over the lip of the window ledge and into the room. Ray was standing on the rug again, his head bowed low. Slowly, Ray started to get undressed, then stopped.

"What do you think you're doing, boy?" his father snapped, making a whistling noise through his nose.

"I'm not doing this anymore," Ray said defiantly.

"You'll do as I tell you," his father insisted.

"Not anymore," Ray said, his voice growing louder.

I watched through the window as Ray stared at his father, those red spots glowing angrily on his forehead and cheeks.

"Don't argue with me, boy," his father commanded.

Ray glanced around the room as if looking for a way of escape – to flee this nightmare. He looked back at his father, who was gawping at him. Ray knew that his father wasn't looking because he had won a fight or done something brave – something he could be proud of. He was staring at him because he was standing in the middle of the living room looking pathetic and weak.

Then, without warning, he turned, rummaged beneath one of the pillows scattered across the sofa, and to my horror he produced a handgun, which he pointed directly at his father's face. I could see that Ray's arm was shaking uncontrollably as he struggled to keep the gun trained on his father's head.

"Don't be stupid, boy. Put the gun down," his father whispered.

"I'm not fucking stupid!" Ray screamed, tears now streaming down his face. *"I'm sick of people calling me stupid!"*

His father visibly flinched as his son screeched at him.

"Okay, okay. You're not stupid. But please put the gun down," his father tried to reason with him.

"You always call me stupid! *Stupid-stupid-stupid!* I'm fucking sick of it!" he roared, spittle flying from his lips.

"Listen, we can sort this..." his father tried to negotiate.

"No! You listen!" Ray screamed and he looked half mad as he waved the gun about.

"Stop! Stop!" his father was pleading now, his hands raised.

The more Ray became upset, the more his hand and arm shook, the gun waving recklessly only inches from his father's face.

"I'm sorry! I'm sorry!" his father began to cry.

"Get on your knees," Ray ordered, his voice wavering.

Sobbing, Ray's father sank to his knees in the middle of

that soft-looking carpet.

"Ever since I can remember, you've hurt me," Ray whispered, trying to keep his voice even. "It stops today, it stops *now*. I'm not a little boy anymore. It was wrong then and it's wrong now."

"Please..." his father whined, snot running from his nose.

"You think you are so brave – a hero," Ray said. "But brave men don't hurt little boys – only cowards do. But the sad thing is, I'm a coward, too. I hurt someone, bullied them because I could – because they were weaker than me – different from me."

As I watched from my hiding place, my heart beat so loud that I feared he might hear it. I knew he was talking about Melody.

"But the thing is," Ray continued, "she wasn't weaker than me, she was stronger – *better* than me. I just wanted to hurt someone. I wanted them to feel like I did. I can be a hero if I want to be – but not like you, dad."

Then Ray slowly lowered the gun and placed it on the floor in front of his father. "I was never going to shoot you. I don't need a gun to feel brave like you do. I'm better than that – I'm better than you."

"Sorry, Ray..." his father snivelled.

Ignoring him, Ray said, "When I was six you told me that I was never to tell mum what you did to me because if I did, you would kill me. So you better make up your mind what you're going to do, because mum will be back soon and I'm going to tell her everything."

His father glanced up at him, his face ashen and old-looking. Tears streamed down his face, but I guessed they weren't for Ray. Then, before I knew what had happened, Ray's father snatched up the gun and was aiming it at his son. Ray didn't flinch or move away. He stood silently and looked down into his father's face. Those few moments of tension were unbearable and I felt as if I was going to throw up.

Ray took two small steps towards his father, so the end of the gun was touching the centre of his chest. "Go on," Ray whispered. "You call yourself a hero."

Then, dropping the gun, Ray's father covered his face with his hands, and rocked slowly back and forth on his knees as he sobbed uncontrollably. Seeing that Ray had finally found the courage to stand up to his father instead of taking his anger out on others, I crept away from the house and into the dark. I kept to the grass verges and I hid in the shadows of the nearby trees as cars passed on the road.

There was one last thing I wanted to do before I left this hell behind me. I wanted to pay Melody's mother a visit.

Chapter Twenty-Two

Isidor

The sky was clear of clouds, and the moon hung yellow and old-looking. It was beautiful like my friends had said it would be, but there was little beauty in this world that I had seen. The house stood on the hill in darkness, a flat, square shape, silhouetted against the moonlight.

Melody's mum's car was nowhere to be seen, so I figured she wasn't back from wherever she had taken Melody to. I pushed open the white wooden gate and it made a wailing noise. I crept up the front garden path. Looking over my shoulder, just to make sure I hadn't been seen, I turned the handle on the front door, but it was locked fast. Not knowing how long I had before she returned, I hurried around the side of the house, checking the first floor windows. They were all locked tight. At the back of the house, I found a wooden cellar doorway set into the ground. It had been padlocked. Glancing around one last time, I flexed my fingers and released my claws. I took the padlock in my fist and crushed it. It fell away and I yanked open the cellar doors. There were a set of stone steps and I followed them down into the darkness. The smell of melted candle wax was overpowering, and I knew that I was in the makeshift chapel where Melody had been punished by her mother. I removed my coat, and spreading my wings, I waited in the darkness for Melody's mum to return.

I don't know how long I waited, but in that darkness, all I could see was Ray pointing that gun at his father. I tried to push those images away, but it was hard to do so. I just wanted to go home and try to forget what I had seen tonight.

It was still dark when I heard the sound of a car pull up and park above me. I heard the front door swing open, and then slam shut. Then, just as I guessed I would, I heard the sound of footsteps on the stairs leading down into the chapel.

I darted across the floor in the dark and hoisted myself

up onto the cross that Melody's mother had put there. I closed my eyes and angled my head forward so my chin was resting against my chest, and cast in shadow.

The sound of a match strike and the smell of sulphur wafted across the chapel. Tilting my head slightly, I opened my eyes a fraction and watched her light two candles. A circular glow of orange light lit the room, and bent forward as if in prayer, she went to a little stone font that I hadn't noticed before. She raised her hands and in the flickering light from the candles, I could see that they were smothered in blood.

My stomach knotted and I felt sick again, as I feared where that blood might have come from. Plunging her hands into the font, she washed away the blood with the holy water. Then dropping to her knees behind one of the pews, she laced her hands together as if in prayer. With her head bowed forward, she said aloud, "Dear Lord, I have sent my wretched child to you for forgiveness. Please release her of her demons, if that is your will."

On hearing her perverted prayer, my heart stopped beating in my chest and the chapel swayed before me. I felt as if I was going to pass out, as I feared Melody had been murdered by her mother.

"Dear sweet Jesus, I pray that you reward me now that I have carried out your will...now that Melody is dead," she said.

Unable to bear any more, I came away from the cross and hovered before her. Hearing the gentle hum of my fluttering wings, she looked up.

"Don't look," I roared. "You're not fit to look upon me."

Her face crumpled with fear, and she dropped to the floor.

"What did you do?" I asked, hovering in the shadows above her so she couldn't see my face.

"What the Lord asked me to do," she muttered. "I killed the demon within my child by sacrificing her."

Hearing this, I landed on the chapel floor and strode towards her, my arms and wings outstretched as if I were about to embrace a small child. I roughly dragged Melody's mother to her feet and held her by her arms.

With my wings beating furiously behind me, she stared at them and whispered, "Are you an angel?"

"Yes," I whispered back, "And your Lord has sent me to deliver a message to you."

"What is his message?" she asked, pounding her chest with her fist.

"He wanted me to tell you, that anyone who hurts a child should kill themselves, rather than face his anger."

I then pushed her away from me, and she looked up into my shadowy face. I could see that hers looked panic-stricken.

"It's not me who is the angel," I roared at her. "It was your daughter and you will burn in Hell for what you have done to her!"

"No!" she screamed, dropping to her knees again. She then started to cover my feet with kisses. "I beg you...please, you must forgive me."

"There is no forgiveness for what you have done," and I didn't like myself for pretending to be a messenger from God, but I hated her. I could have ripped out her heart with my claws, and the urge to do so was overpowering. But I wanted her to spend every second of every day, fearing the moment she would die and face the God that she believed in. There was a spike of anger that knifed its way through my soul and I couldn't do anything to stop the pain that it caused.

"There must be some way that I can redeem myself, a way so that I can enter God's kingdom someday," she pleaded on her knees.

I kicked her off me, and with my wings casting long shadows all around us, I said, "Sacrifice yourself. That is the only way you will ever enter his kingdom."

I then left her sobbing on the chapel floor, full of self-pity and no remorse for killing Melody.

The first rays of sunlight cut through the clouds, and as I stumbled back across the fields, I dropped to my knees. Pounding my fists into the earth over and over again, I screamed. I threw my head back and roared up at the sky until my throat was raw.

"I hate you!" I screamed. *"I hate you!"*

With tears of anger gushing down my face, I raced up into the sky. Tearing through the clouds I wanted to fly as high as I could. I wanted to come face to face with the humans' God. When the air became so thin and cold that I thought I was going to lose consciousness, I hovered above the clouds, my wings rippling beneath my arms.

"Show yourself to me!" I screamed up into the heavens. *"Go on, you chicken shit!"*

The wind buffeted me from side to side.

"What sort of God lets shit like this happen?" I roared. *"What kinda God would let Ray's father hurt him like that? What sort of God would have allowed Melody to die?"*

The wind dragged me left then right, almost as if it were trying to play with me, like a child when it plays with a ragdoll.

"There is no God. There is no heaven," I muttered. Then, looking down at the Earth, I whispered, "There is only Hell."

Lowering my arms and placing them against my sides, I dropped back through the clouds like a stone. Melody's necklace whipped about my chest as I fell. Within inches of the ground, I snapped open my arms and soared away. I just wanted to go home, back to The Hollows.

Chapter Twenty-Three

Isidor

I dropped through the canopy of trees that sheltered the woods. In the distance I could smell the fresh water of the lake, but I couldn't go back there, not now. I stretched out my wings and tensed my muscles. My wings didn't disappear, they just hung there. Inspecting my arms, I could see that those purple scars had gone, leaving my wings permanently on show. They were a part of me. Maybe they didn't want to hide anymore? Perhaps they wanted to be free. My mother had said they would get stuck someday if I used them too much, and it looked as if she had been right all along.

I made my way through the woods to the grate and the tunnel that would lead me home. The grate was hidden by a blanket of leaves and twigs. On my knees, I brushed them aside and then stopped, my hand hovering above the grate. Someone had placed a folded piece of paper between the slits. With my heart racing, I pulled the paper from the grate and unfolded it. It wasn't a piece of paper at all, but a photograph. I looked at it and stumbled backwards onto my arse. Sitting amongst the damp leaves that covered the ground, I stared down at the photograph of Melody and me. But we looked different – we looked a few years older – late teens, maybe? We had our arms around each other, both of us staring into the camera lens. Melody looked beautiful, her hair free and flowing about her shoulders, as if caught in a gentle breeze. I could see those roses covering her arms and neck, bright and red and pink and full of life. But I had tattoos, too. They looked like black flames seething up my left arm and neck. There was a little stubby black beard covering my chin, and an eyebrow piercing in my right brow. Around my neck, not only hung Melody's rosary beads, but several others, and in my hand I carried a crossbow.

I didn't have to wonder who had left the picture for me; I knew it was Melody who had somehow placed it there. I had given her the idea. Just like Steve Edwards had in the story that I had written for Melody, I sat and looked at the picture. But it wasn't of Michael Blake amongst a screaming crowd of adoring Marilyn Monroe fans; it was a picture of Melody and me from another time, another place – another *when*. But just like Michael had in the postcard he'd left for Edwards, Melody and I looked happy at last.

I turned the photograph over, and across the back she had written the word *PUSH!*

Chapter Twenty-Four

Kiera

Isidor had talked throughout the night. Dawn was fast approaching, but the storm still raged outside, and the heavy, black clouds gave the impression that it was still night. Isidor suddenly stopped talking, and apart from the sound of the wind screaming outside and the sudden burst of thunder, the waiting room had fallen into a hushed silence.

Isidor sat across from me, his head down, crossbow in his lap. His story had left me feeling shocked and upset, and I looked around the waiting room at the others. Kayla sat at the end of the bench where Sam still lay asleep, and Potter sat on the floor, his back against the wall. I think all of us had been affected by Isidor's story. Kayla slowly got up from her seat, and sitting next to Isidor, she put her arm around his shoulder.

"I'm so sorry, Isidor, that you lost Melody," she said.

"I didn't lose her, she was murdered," Isidor said numbly. "Sometimes, I miss her so much that I wish I had never met her. I went above ground for an adventure, to see those faces in the clouds, to feel the sun against me, to watch cars pass by, and see those machines that soar through the sky. But instead, I only discovered monsters."

"Not all humans are monsters..." I started, but before I could finish Isidor cut in.

"Sometimes, Kiera, I wish you had made that decision back in The Hollows and chosen the Vampyrus to live!" he shouted.

"Isidor, you don't really mean that," I whispered.

"My mother told me if the humans found out that I was different to them, they would cut me open to see how I worked," he snapped. "But it's not the Vampyrus who are the monsters – it's the humans."

"But, Isidor, like me, you are a half and half," I said softly, understanding his anger and frustration.

"And that's what I can't reconcile," he said. "I hate myself for being part human."

"But you fell in love with a human," Potter said, staring at Isidor. "Melody wasn't evil. You yourself said she was an angel."

"And now she's a dead angel, thanks to a human," he said bitterly.

No one said anything for a while after this. When the silence became too uncomfortable to bear, and wanting to know more about the picture that Melody had left in the grate for Isidor, I looked at him and asked, "Have you still got that photograph?"

Without saying a word, Isidor reached inside his coat and pulled out a folded piece of paper. He handed it to me. Taking it very carefully in my hands, as I knew it must have been very special to him, I unfolded the picture. It was Isidor, just as he looked now. He stood beside the girl he had called Melody and she was beautiful – how could anyone have ever thought otherwise? Her long, blond hair was just how Isidor had described it, long, thick, and curly. Her arms were covered in the most realistic tattoos. The roses looked almost real, as if they were swaying in a gentle breeze that was obviously blowing around Melody and Isidor in the photo. I could have stared at those tattoos for hours, believing at any moment those roses were going to open and flower. Then, turning the photo over in my hands, I saw the word *PUSH!* which had been written in ink across the back.

Handing the picture to Potter, I looked at Isidor and said, "So you have no idea where that picture was taken?"

"No," he said, shaking his head.

"So you haven't met up with her since she was driven away that day by her mum?" Potter asked, inspecting the photo.

"I've told you already that she is dead," Isidor said.

"But the tattoos," Kayla breathed, peering over Potter's shoulder at the picture. "You must have seen her again since having your tattoos done."

"I had those done because of the photograph," Isidor

said, taking the picture from Potter and placing it carefully back into his coat pocket.

"What do you mean?" I asked him.

"I was so desperate to see Melody again, that I did everything that I could think of to make sure that day would come," he told us. "So I went and had the tattoos done. I took the photograph along to the tattooist. He worked from the picture. I then had my eyebrow pierced and trained myself in the art of using a crossbow. I didn't know why I needed to do any of these things, but that's how I looked in that photograph – so I made sure I copied it."

"So you never met with her again?" Potter asked a second time.

"Look, how many ways have I got to tell you?" Isidor sighed. "I've not seen Melody since the day her mother snatched her away from me. She's dead."

"But she can't be," Kayla said. "She's in that picture with you and you're very much alive."

Then, looking at the three of them, I gasped and said, "But that's the whole point don't you see? We're not alive – we're dead."

Isidor looked at me, and leaning forward on the bench, he said, "You mean Melody might be here? Just because she's dead in the other world, it doesn't mean that she is dead here."

"This world has been *pushed*," Kayla gasped. "That's what she was trying to say when she wrote that word across the back of the picture!"

I listened to what Kayla had said, and I thought of my own dad. He was dead in the other world – but what about here? He could still be alive! I looked at Potter and our eyes fixed on one another's momentarily.

As if knowing what I was thinking, he looked at me and said, "Don't go getting any funny ideas, Kiera."

"What do you mean by that?" I asked him.

"All I'm trying to say is, don't give Isidor false hope," he said, lighting up a cigarette. "Just because that girl died before the world got *pushed*, it doesn't mean that she is alive here."

"But what about my dad..." I started.

"Don't go there, Kiera," he cut over me. "You'll only get hurt."

"How can you be so sure?" I asked him with a frown.

"I'm not sure about anything, but we haven't come back to go waking the dead," he said, and sucked on the end of his cigarette.

"But he might not be dead..."

Again Potter spoke over me and said, "Look, we don't know anything for sure and raising ghosts isn't what I call a good idea."

I looked at Potter and I got a feeling that perhaps he knew more about this world, which had been *pushed,* than he was telling me.

"What I want to know is," Kayla piped up, "how did the photograph end up in that grate if it came from this world which has been *pushed*?"

"How should I freaking know?" Potter shrugged, blowing out a mouthful of smoke.

"Pictures, postcards and stuff like that shouldn't be able to slip between the two different worlds, should they?" she asked him.

Potter paused for a moment, as if he had been slapped across the face. Then, recovering quickly, he barked, "Why are you asking me? I don't know every goddamn thing."

Again, I got that sinking feeling that he was keeping something from us.

But before I'd the chance to question him further, Potter turned on Isidor and said, "So, you sure you didn't see Melody again?"

"No," Isidor insisted. "After what happened to Melody, I spent most of my time on my own. I felt utterly lost without her being around. I looked at the picture constantly, and in my heart I knew that one day we would meet each other again. We had to – we were in the picture together. I just didn't know where or *when* that would be. A couple of years later, I was about sixteen, I went back to the lake and the bushes where we had our camp. To my surprise, I found one of the old eyeliners that Melody had stolen from the shop, and the comic she had first brought me. They were hidden in the camp beneath some dry leaves and twigs. But it wasn't the same without Melody. I would wait for hours, sometimes days hoping she would come back, just like the photograph suggested she would. Eventually, it became too painful to go there.

"I returned to The Hollows, where I would lie on my bed writing stories and rereading that comic she had given to me. But in my heart, I just couldn't stop wondering where Melody was or what she was doing. I just hoped she was happy. I only went back to look for Melody once more, and that time, I went to the house where she had lived with her mum.

"The windows were all boarded over. The front garden was overgrown with weeds and wildflowers. The house looked derelict and abandoned. I wanted to know what had happened, so I returned to the library and checked the local newspapers. I didn't have to look for very long, as I soon came across an article about a local woman who had hung herself in a chapel constructed in the basement of her house. There was other stuff written about her but I didn't need to read it. I knew she had sacrificed herself in search of the redemption she hoped to find. Did I feel bad about what had happened to her? No more than she felt bad about punishing her daughter in that chapel," Isidor said.

"But what about that word *Pushed*?" I asked again. "How did she know about that?"

Before anyone had a chance to even consider the answer to my question, Kayla had placed a finger over her lips and said, "Shhh!"

We all watched as she went to the window and peered out.

"What's wrong?" I whispered.

"I can hear them coming," she said, staring out into the dark.

"Hear who?" Potter asked.

"Those Berserkers, and there's a lot of them," she said, turning to look at us, her eyes wide.

Chapter Twenty-Five

Kiera

I could only hear the wind howling through the nearby valleys and over the hills. My hearing wasn't as sensitive as Kayla's, but I had no reason to doubt her. I raced across the waiting room, and easing her to one side, I peered out into the darkness.

With the hairs prickling at the base of my neck, I could see a mass of dark shadows as they poured into the valley like liquid black. They moved fast, like a huge wave cascading over the hills and flooding the valley that the station sat in.

"We're in trouble," I breathed, turning away from the window and looking at the others.

"What kinda trouble?" Potter asked, his fangs, claws, and wings already out. He stood in the pale light of the waiting room, like a winged demon, his claws so big that the ivory nails swung below his knees. His eyes had turned so black that I could no longer see the pupils.

"There are lots of them, and they're heading this way - and fast," I told him, releasing my own claws, wings, and fangs. My wings hummed on either side of me, those bony black fingers snatching at the air.

"What's that?" Kayla suddenly asked, going back to the window, her wings shimmering as if sprayed with glitter.

"What's what?" Potter snapped, the tension in the waiting room rising.

Tilting her head to one side, Kayla looked back at us and said, "I can hear a train coming."

"How far away is it?" I asked, peering over her shoulder and into the night.

"It's closer than those berserkers are," Kayla whispered, her eyes wide and full of fear.

Potter went to the door, opened it, and stepped out onto the platform. A gust of wind howled into the waiting room, blowing Kayla's red hair back from her face like an explosion of flames.

"The train is close, but so are those berserkers," Potter barked as he raced back into the waiting room. "Which of them gets here first is anyone's guess, but let's be ready. Wake the wolf-boy, Kayla."

I looked across the waiting room at Isidor. He sat on the bench, his head low and crossbow placed across his lap. "Isidor?" I said, surprised that he wasn't standing with his wings out and crossbow at the ready. "Isidor, the Berserkers are coming. We've got to get out of here, and quick," I said, hoping this would stir him.

Then, raising his head to look at me, he said, "Kiera, I'm not coming with you."

"Listen, kid, we don't have time to fuck about," Potter said, glancing at him, but keeping one eye on the door. "Get your shit together, we're moving out."

"I'm not coming," Isidor said again.

The wind roared outside, and rattled the windows in their frames. A rumble of thunder boomed so loud in the distance that the waiting room shook in its foundations.

"Come on, Isidor," I pushed, "the storm is getting worse. We've got to go."

"That wasn't the sound of the storm you just heard," Kayla gasped, "that was the Berserkers you could hear."

I snapped my head around and looked through the open doorway. With my eyes like two narrow slits, I peered into the distance and could now see the Berserkers racing through the valley towards the station. Their howling and snarling was like a monstrous chorus, as all of them charged towards us. Knowing that we had just minutes to make our escape, I looked left and could see the headlight of a train heading out of the night towards us.

I turned to look at Isidor, who was still seated. With very little time to waste, I darted towards him and took hold of his wrist in my claws. "Get up," I snapped at him. "You're coming with us."

"I'm staying," he said softly as he looked into my eyes.

"Say what?" Kayla gasped, as if she had only just realised that Isidor was being serious. "You can't stay. There are so many of those Berserkers..."

"You go," Isidor smiled kindly at his sister. "I'll stay and draw them away so you can escape."

"No!" Kayla snapped, trying to yank him off the bench.

"Please, Kayla," Isidor said. "I want to do this."

"I don't want you to," Kayla cried, and I could see tears beginning to stand in her eyes. "I'm not leaving without you."

With an uncharacteristic look of concern on his face, Potter came forward, and moving Kayla aside, he looked down at Isidor and said, "Are you for fucking real?"

"I want to stay," Isidor said, looking back at him.

"Why?" Potter asked his voice now full of concern.

"You don't need me," Isidor explained. "You've got Kiera and Kiera has you. Kayla has Sam. Who do I have?"

"You have your friends," Potter said, holding out his hand for Isidor to take.

"It's not enough," Isidor said over the sound of the approaching Berserkers. "I'm tired."

"Tired of what?" I asked, not believing what I was hearing.

"Tired of having no real place in the team," Isidor said. "I don't bring anything to the party. I never solve the mystery – I just provide the laughs – I'm Shaggy-Doo."

Potter stared at Isidor, then flashing his fangs; he gripped Isidor by his arm and dragged him from his seat. "Like it or not, Isidor, you're coming with us. I'm not leaving here without you."

With a wild snarl like I had never heard come from Isidor before, he pushed Potter off him and drew his crossbow. Aiming it at Potter, he hissed, "I'm not coming! Now go – all of you!"

"Isidor, *please!*" Kayla cried out, throwing herself at him. With her arms wrapped about his waist, she began to sob. "Please come with us. You're my brother. *I love you.*"

"I love you, too," Isidor whispered, tears spilling onto his cheeks. "But that's why I'm staying. I don't want to run anymore. I'll draw the Berserkers' attention so you can get away."

"But they'll kill you," she sobbed, holding him tighter.

"I'm already dead," he whispered back. "I have been, since Melody was taken from me that day. I hoped that I would find something to fill the hole that she left inside of me – but I never have. Let me just do this one thing for the team. I'll catch you up – I promise."

"No, that's not true," she cried against him.

"Go, Kayla," he said, easing her gently off him. "Save your friend Sam. Get him to the Fountain of Souls. You have him now; aren't I entitled to have a special friend, too?"

As if knowing that Isidor wasn't going to be persuaded to come with us, and the Berserkers just moments away, Potter stepped forward and took Kayla in his arms. Smoothing out her hair with his claws, he whispered, "Kayla, get Sam onto the platform, because when that train comes steaming through, we need to be on it."

"I can't," she sobbed in Potter's arms.

"You have to," he whispered back, guiding her over to the bench where Sam lay.

Crying softly, Kayla scooped Sam up into her arms and carried him from the waiting room, not once looking back at her brother.

With the sound of the train roaring towards us, and the yapping and howling of the Berserkers growing ever nearer, I looked at Isidor and said, "You don't have anything to prove. You are part of our team – part of our family."

"I have to stay and wait for Melody," Isidor said, taking the picture of them from his coat pocket again.

"But the Berserkers will kill you while you wait for her," I tried desperately to convince him.

"But don't you see?" he said holding up the picture. "The Berserkers can't kill me because this picture hasn't been taken yet. The fact that it exists says that I'm not going to die today."

"But..." I started.

"I'm so tired of waiting – hoping that the moment this picture was taken comes," he said. "So maybe by waiting for the Berserkers, it will force her hand and she'll come for me."

"Please..." I started again, but couldn't finish, as my lower lip trembled and tears trickled down my cheeks. I took a deep breath as I tried to steady myself, and looking at him, I said one last time, "Come with us, Isidor."

Staring back at me, a look of determination drawn over his face, Isidor said, "Run, Kiera, or you're gonna miss your train."

Knowing that I would never get him to change his mind, I crossed the waiting room and held him tightly in my arms. "I love you, Isidor," I whispered and kissed him softly on his cheek. "See you later, alligator."

"In a while, crocodile," he whispered back.

Then, letting go of him, I ran across the waiting room, snatched up the rucksacks, and ran out onto the platform.

Chapter Twenty-Six

Isidor

"Shouldn't you be going, too?" I asked Potter, as he stood before me in the waiting room.

"Why are you doing this?" Potter asked with a frown.

"Because I want to see Melody again," I answered.

Taking two steps towards me, so we were just inches apart, Potter spoke in a hushed voice and said, "Isidor, believe it or not, I know what it feels like to have a broken heart. I loved a girl once but she's gone now, and in a way, it was the best thing that could have happened to me, because I would've never met Kiera."

"But I haven't met anyone else, that's my point," I tried to explain. "I don't have anybody. Melody hasn't gone, she is here somewhere, we will meet again – the picture proves that."

Then, glancing quickly back over his shoulder then back at me, Potter whispered, "I know about pictures and stuff that seem to have been *pushed* between the two worlds, and no good will come of it."

"What are you talking about?" I asked him.

"I don't have time to explain," he said, glancing back over his shoulder. "But believe me, Isidor, that picture of you and Melody, just like the letters that got *pushed* over to the girl I once loved, only led to suffering, and eventually, her death. Please come with us, Isidor, I don't want to leave you behind."

"I'm staying, Potter, I know what I'm doing," I told him.

With the rickety old waiting room now lurching from side to side in the growing storm, and the sound of the approaching train and Berserkers nearly upon us, Potter looked at me and said, "I'm sorry, Isidor. I never meant to put you down or hurt you. You are my friend – you're my brother."

To hear him say that meant more to me than anything. It made me want to cry with happiness, but just like Melody had said to me once, I just couldn't let it show. With a smile

145

pulling at the corner of my mouth, I held out my hand for him to shake and said, "I know – but just like all older brothers, I guess someday you've got to let your younger brother find his own way."

Potter glanced down at my hand, but instead of shaking it, he came forward and hugged me so tight that I thought he was going to shatter every one of my ribs. "I'm sorry," he whispered.

Then releasing his grip on me, he took a cigarette from his trouser pocket, and tucked it behind my ear.

"But I don't smoke," I told him.

"It's for Melody," he said softly, then he turned and left me standing alone in the waiting room.

I heard the train slow as it passed through the station, and I hoped Kayla and my friends had managed to get on board. The driver blew on the horn as the train started to speed up. The wind screamed and howled outside and the door to the waiting room rattled in its frame. Then caught in a sudden gust of wind, the door flew open, snatching the photograph of Melody and me from my hand. It flew into the air, seesawed momentarily so I could get one last glimpse of us together, then it fluttered out of the open doorway and up into the grey dawn sky. I raced to the door, but it was gone.

I looked to my right and could see the train speeding out of the station, and to my left I saw the first of the Berserkers leap onto the platform. This was the first time that I had seen them – and they didn't really look like wolves at all – they looked as if they had been trapped halfway between wolf and human – just how Sam now looked. They bounded up the platform on all fours towards me. Their claws made a clacking sound against the ground. Sniffing at the air, they looked at me with their seething eyes and snarled. With their half-human faces and flesh coloured snouts, they rolled back their lips and brandished their razor-like teeth at me

Turning, I went back into the waiting room and closed the door behind me. I knew that it wouldn't hold them back for long, if at all. The old fashioned-looking radio that I had first noticed on the counter by the tiny ticket booth made a crackling sound. I moved towards it, and I could clearly hear the sound of static. Picking it up, I pressed my ear flat against it and closed my eyes. In the hiss of the static, I was sure I could hear the faint sound of music and it was growing louder. With hands beginning to tremble, I realised I had heard that song before; it was the song that Melody and I used to sit and listen to down by Lake Lure. As the music grew louder and clearer, I began to hum along to *Heroes* by David Bowie.

With the music now filling the waiting room in a thick wall of sound, I set the radio down and looked back over my shoulder at the door. It slowly swung open, and in the doorway were several of those Berserkers. They were no longer on all fours, but standing upright like men. With giant paws that swung against their knees, they walked towards me. I looked into their burning eyes, and each of them opened their drooling jaws and roared.

Turning my back on them, it was then I noticed those levers again – the ones with the words *push* and *pull* written above them in faded-out letters. Just as if I'd been punched in the face, the word which had been written on the back of the photograph flashed in the front of my mind.

With the Berserker's breath hot against my neck and the song *Heroes* now blasting from the radio at an ear-splitting level, I closed my eyes and gripped the lever which had *PUSH* written above it. And as I did, I felt the Berserker's claws slice through my neck. But there was one last sensation I felt before the world went black. I felt a hand softly close over mine, the one that had just *pushed* the lever.

Chapter Twenty-Seven

Kiera

Potter came from the waiting room and joined us on the platform. He had a look on his face that I had only ever seen once before, and that had been as he cradled Murphy's dead body in his arms beneath the Fountain of Souls. Like me, Potter knew that we would never see Isidor again – the Berserkers would kill him.

To see such hurt on Potter's face, and feeling as if my soul had been crushed, I headed back down the platform towards the waiting room. I was going to take Isidor with us, even if it meant dragging him kicking and screaming. As I passed Potter, he grabbed my arm.

"Don't," he whispered, tears in his eyes.

"But we can't just leave him," I cried, glancing at Kayla who had rested Sam down on the platform. Kayla stood with her head down and was hugging herself. I didn't need to see her face to know that she was crying, her shuddering shoulders told me that.

"Isidor needs to find his own path," Potter said softly. "I just hope he finds Melody at the end of it."

I tried to move off in the direction of the waiting room again, but Potter held onto me. "We don't have time. We can't risk all of our lives because of Isidor."

Not wanting to hear what Potter had said, but knowing what he said was true, I looked at Kayla. I went to her and wrapped my arm about her shoulder. Then, as if getting his act together, Potter came charging towards us, picked Sam up off the platform, and barked, "We don't have time for all this booing and wooing, save it for later."

The train slowed as it reached the platform, but didn't stop. The Berserkers were so close now that I could hear their barking and yapping from the opposite end of the platform. With Sam hanging over his shoulder like a ragdoll, Potter raced alongside the train as it passed through the platform.

"C'mon!" he yelled back at Kayla and me.

With my arm still firmly around her shoulder, I hurried Kayla alongside the train. It was a goods train, and one of the cars had a wide open door. Seeing this, Potter raced beside it and shoved Sam into the opening. With Kayla on a go slow, we were beginning to trail behind, and I looked up to see Potter leap from the platform and into the car.

"Hurry!" he roared, his claws outstretched towards us.

"Faster," I yelled at Kayla who stumbled beside me.

"I don't want to leave Isidor..." she started.

But before she had the chance to protest further, Potter had snatched hold of her wrists with his claws and was yanking her up and into the carriage. Her hair blew backwards like a streak of flame and the sky rumbled overhead.

"Take my hand!" Potter barked at me, as I raced alongside the train. "Take hold!"

Reaching out, our claws joined and he hauled me on board. The train lurched right as it rattled over the points at the end of the platform. Taking hold of a handrail fixed to the giant door, I looked out and back at the station. With the wind blasting into my face, I watched in horror as the Berserkers ran along the platform like a plague of giant locusts. They pulled the waiting room door open and hurried inside.

With my stomach aching like I'd been winded, I peered into the darkness and through the window set into the wall of the waiting room. Stifling a scream with my fists, I watched as the Berserkers circled Isidor. Why did he have his back to them?

Fight, Isidor! Turn and fight! I wanted to scream over the sound of the roaring wind, but the words wouldn't come out. Then, one of those Berserkers swiped its claws through the air, slicing Isidor's head from his shoulders. With blood slashing against the waiting room window, I sunk to my knees as the Berserkers set about Isidor's body with their claws and dagger-like teeth.

Potter pulled me into the car and slid the door shut, as we sped away from the station and up into the snow-flecked mountains.

Chapter Twenty-Eight

Isidor

The hand which held mine felt soft, delicate. Slowly, I opened my eyes and peered down at the rose which covered the back of it. With my heart racing in my chest, I looked up into the face which smiled back at me and two things struck me all at once. My heart was beating again in my chest, a feeling that I hadn't felt since coming back from the dead and into the world which had been *pushed*. The second thing, my arms and hands felt different – lighter somehow – and I didn't have to inspect them to know that I no longer had wings or claws.

I looked into her eyes and they were more beautiful than I had remembered them – Melody had become more beautiful. She looked just like she had in that photograph. She was no longer that uncomfortable fourteen-year-old girl in the grey dress, apron, and bonnet. Melody stood before me, her long, blonde hair curled around her shoulders like springs made of silk. Just as she had in the photograph, she wore a sleeveless summer dress which swished just above her knees. The rose tattoos covered her legs, arms, and neck, and they looked so real that I had to fight the urge to lean forward and smell their sweet scent.

I had been too busy staring at Melody to realise that I was standing in a waiting room similar to the one I had just left. There was a tiny ticket booth, and a series of levers attached to the wall. But instead of benches, there were tables and chairs, like a small café where travellers could sit, eat, and drink while they waited for their train. As I glanced around this old fashioned-looking waiting room, I could see people seated at the tables. There was a teenage couple, and they sat across a table from each other, gazing into one another's eyes. I could see that they were very much in love. There was a woman seated at a table nearby, and she was real pretty. Her hair was so blond that it looked almost white. She wore a long, brown coat with a fur collar and was busy reading a bunch of letters that were piled on the table before her. She looked familiar, very much like the pathologist I'd seen in the morgue where I had rescued Kiera from. But that would be impossible, right? There were two other people that I could see. One was male, and he looked ill. His skin was waxy-looking and his eyes were jet black. He stared down at his arm, and the skin covering it looked wrinkled and worn. The other one, I couldn't tell if it were male or female, as a hood was pulled so low, that it hid the face.

I looked back at Melody again, she was still holding my hand and my heart was still pounding. Then, I did something that I had longed to do since her mother had taken her away four years ago. Pulling her close to me, I leaned forward and kissed her. Melody wrapped her arms around my neck and kissed me back. Her lips were as soft and sweet tasting as those roses which covered her body.

Gently easing our lips apart, I brushed a loose strand of hair from her cheek and said, "I love you, Melody."

"I love you more," she smiled at me, and I thought my heart was going to burst from my chest.

From beside us, someone said, "Aww, how beautiful you two look together. I must take a photo."

Both of us looked in the direction of the voice at the same time, and there was a flash of white light. I blinked, and when I looked again, I could see that it was the person who had been seated at the table with the hood who had taken our picture. The hooded person lowered the camera, but still their face was hidden from me by the folds of the grey coloured hood.

Without saying another word, the hooded figure turned and strode towards the waiting room door.

"Hey!" I called out, realising whoever hid behind the hood had just taken the picture I had carried around with me for so long. "I need that picture."

The hooded figure turned back and looked at me. "I have other pictures, Isidor Smith," it said, and its voice sounded so cracked and broken, that I still couldn't tell if it were male or female. "And I don't just have pictures; I have letters and all sorts of other stuff for the friends you've left behind."

The door to the waiting room creaked as the person with the camera stepped outside. Letting go of Melody's hand, I decided to follow. I yanked open the door and stepped out onto the platform that had been constructed from wood. It was old, and the boards wailed beneath me. I raised my hand against the bright sunlight that shimmered from above. Snapping my head left, then right, I looked for the person with the camera, but the hooded figure had gone – vanished somehow. In each direction, all I could see was a flat landscape. The ground was the colour of sand, but it was cracked and arid-looking and stretched for miles in all directions.

Melody joined me on the platform. "What's wrong, Isidor?"

"We need to find whoever that was who just took our picture," I told her. "We need that photograph."

"Why?" she asked, taking my hand again.

"Because you leave it for me in that grate," I said. "You wrote *push* on the back of it. If you hadn't have written that, I would never have pushed that lever and I wouldn't be here with you now."

With a frown, Melody looked at me and said, "Isidor, I never left any picture for you. I never wrote that word on anything."

"But you left me the photo so I would find you here," I told her, and now my heart was beginning to race for a different reason.

"I never left a photo for you, Isidor," she said again, looking as confused as I felt.

"Who did then?" I breathed.

"Whoever wanted you dead, I guess," Melody said.

"Dead?" I whispered.

"You're dead, Isidor," she said. "Whoever left you the photo and wrote *push* on the back, led you here."

With my heart racing faster and faster, I realised I had been tricked. The photograph had been used as bait to lure me to my own death. But whoever had taken that picture had said that there were other photographs for my friends. Did that mean that they were going to be lured to their own deaths too? I had to warn them.

"I have to go back," I said.

"You can't, Isidor," Melody called after me as I raced back into the waiting room.

I yanked on the levers that were attached to the wall. I pushed them then pulled them, but nothing happened. "Why am I still here?" I cried out.

"Isidor, there is no way back, you're dead. We both are," Melody said softly. "It's hard for everyone to accept at first, as this place seems so real, but..."

"I've got to go back and warn my friends, my sister, not to be fooled by photographs of those they miss the most," I said, yanking at the levers.

"There is no way back," she said, taking my hand again. "You'll get used to it. I was scared at first, but it does get easier."

"You don't understand, Melody," I cried.

"Not at first I didn't," she said. "I couldn't believe that my mother stabbed me in the heart, only to find myself sitting here at this station."

With the sudden realisation I was dead – dead for real this time – with no chance of returning to the world that had been *pushed* or any other world, I began to tremble. But not out of fear for myself, but that of my friends. Who was the person behind the hood, the person who had tricked me with that picture?

As if sensing my fear, Melody smiled at me, and said, "Come with me, Isidor, we can catch the next train now."

"The next train?" I asked her, feeling lost.

"I've been waiting here for you all this time," she smiled at me and squeezed my hand.

Then, leading me back across the waiting room, we went back out onto the platform. There was a wailing sound from above and I looked up to see a sign swinging in the wind on a set of rusty hinges.

The Great Wasteland Railroad, it read.

Sitting together on the platform, with my crossbow on my lap, we held hands and waited for the next train to take us away.

Chapter Twenty-Nine

Kiera

The train rattled its way through the mountain passes and over bridges that spanned giant valleys. With the door open just an inch or two, I sat silently and watched the cold, winter sun rise above the storm clouds which were fading away into the distance.

Kayla had cried herself to sleep and lay on the dusty floor next to her friend Sam. Every so often, Sam would stir and cry out in his feverish stupor. Potter sat with his back against the wall of the carriage and smoked. We didn't speak. I wanted to ask him if he were keeping secrets from me, but now wasn't the time. I was still in shock from seeing Isidor get slaughtered by those Berserkers. And as I pictured them in my mind's eye as they approached Isidor from behind, I glanced over at Sam. He looked like one of them.

Closing my eyes, I let the cold air which blasted through the gap in the door cool my face. I thought of the photograph Isidor had carried with him. He had been wrong about that picture. Even though he was in the photograph with Melody, he had died before meeting up with her again. As I sat, feeling the rocking sensation of the train as it raced forward, I suddenly got a sinking feeling in the pit of my stomach.

I opened my eyes and looked for the rucksack I'd brought with me from Hallowed Manor. Reaching out, I dragged it across the floor of the carriage towards me. Then with my hands shaking, I unfastened it and reached inside. With my fingers brushing over the picture of my dad and me, which Potter had taken from my flat in Havensfield, I sat and stared at it. Gooseflesh ran over my skin as I realised what was wrong with the photograph.

I couldn't ever remember that particular photograph being taken. If I couldn't remember it being taken, then it never had been – not yet, anyway. The reason why I couldn't remember posing for that picture with my dad was because, like Isidor's photograph, it hadn't been taken yet. So how was I holding it in my hands?

"Are you okay, sweet-cheeks?" Potter suddenly asked me.

"No, not really," I whispered, unable to take my eyes from the photograph in the frame.

Potter came and sat beside me. "What's wrong?"

"This picture's wrong – it's all wrong," I told him.

"It's just a picture of you and your dad," he said, and again there was a dismissive tone to his voice, which made me wonder if he were hiding something from me.

"It's not just a photo," I said, looking at him, wanting to see the reaction in his eyes. "This picture hasn't been taken yet."

Potter broke my stare and looked down at the photograph. He didn't say anything, not at first. "You're in it."

"But I don't ever remember having this picture taken," I told him, not taking my eyes from his.

"You could never remember all the photographs that you've ever been in," he tried to reason with me.

"My dad had jet-black hair," I told him. "In this picture, he has wisps of grey – he is older looking in this picture than when he died."

"So what are you trying to say?" Potter asked, and again he didn't make eye contact and lit another cigarette.

"My dad is alive in this world, and this picture proves I meet up with him again," I whispered, praying that it was true – that I was going to see my dad again. If I had a heart it would have been racing with joy.

"Kiera, I found that picture in your flat," Potter said, exasperated. "You would have never known about it if I hadn't have gone and got it for you. That picture holds no significance to what we've been brought back to do. It's a fluke that you're even holding it now."

I sat and stared down at the picture. Then, with my fist, I smashed the glass and removed the photograph from its frame and turned it over in my hands.

"I was meant to have this picture," I whispered. "It's a sign."

"What are you talking about, Kiera?" Potter sighed.

I held up the picture with my trembling hands and showed him what had been written across the back. Someone had scribbled just one word, and it read, *PUSH*.

'Dead Statues'

Book Three Kiera Hudson Series Two
Coming soon!

Author's Note:

Isidor told Melody about his dream to write stories. He called them his *Penny Dreadfuls* – because he feared they would be so dreadful people wouldn't even spend a penny of their money buying them. Shortly after Isidor's death at that remote Railway Station, I woke one morning to find a brown envelope stuffed through my letterbox. I opened it to find four short stories. They were called, *"There Are tigers"*, *"Ratbag"*, *"Paisley End"* and *"A Story"*. These were the stories which Isidor wrote between the ages of fourteen to sixteen. After reading each of these dark little tales, I could see that each had been inspired by what Isidor had seen and learnt about the humans during his adventures above ground. When checking the envelope to see if there was any sign or clue as to who had sent them to me, there was only one word scrawled across the front...

Over the page you will find that collection of short stories by Isidor Smith.

The Penny Dreadfuls

By
Isidor Smith

For Melody Rose

'There Are tigers'

"Don't go home via the underpass," she said, looking at her grandson.

"Why not, Nan?" Michael asked.

"There are tigers beneath that underpass," the old woman said, her false teeth loosening around her withered gums.

"Tigers?" Michael said, his stomach tightening at the sight of his grandmother rearranging her teeth with a grey coloured tongue. "There ain't no tigers beneath the underpass."

"Calling your poor old Nan a liar, are you?" she said, fixing him with a beady stare.

Shuffling from foot to foot, Michael snatched up his rucksack and threw it over his shoulder. "Nah, I'm not calling you a liar – it's just that I can't believe there are..."

"Children have gone missing," the old woman cut in, her bones creaking as she sat further back in her armchair. "Boys and girls the same age as you – gone, disappeared, never to be seen again."

With a nervous smile tugging at the corners of his mouth, Michael said, "Nan, I'm not six anymore – I'm fourteen. You can't scare me with your ghost stories."

"It isn't a ghost story, Mikey," she said, pointing at him with a finger that was crooked and bent out of shape. "There are tigers beneath that underpass. They hide in the shadows – no one ever sees them until it's too late."

"Ah c'mon, Nan!" Michael groaned as he headed for the door. "I aint afraid of no gang of hoodies. That group of low-lives that hang around beneath the underpass don't scare me."

"They're tigers!" the old woman croaked, her voice sounding rasping and old.

Glancing back over his shoulder, Michael looked at his grandmother and said, "That gang of hoodies can call themselves the Black Panthers for all I care. I ain't scared of 'em." Without saying another word, Michael yanked open the front door and left his grandmother's house. There was a clicking sound and Michael wasn't sure whether it was the sound of the latch locking as he shut the door behind him, or the sound of his grandmother pushing her false teeth back into place with her tongue.

Pulling the collar of his blazer about his neck, Michael lowered his head against the rain that spattered his face like needlepoints. The streets were dark and deserted as he made his way across town to his home. The rain hissed as it bounced off the pavement and tarmac. The sound reminded him of Clarence the family cat, spitting and hissing at the dog that lived next door. Listening to that sound and the thought of the family pet made his mind wander to thoughts of bigger cats – tigers, in fact.

There are tigers beneath that underpass!

Michael could hear his Nan's voice in his head.

"Poor, old Nan," he whispered to himself, as he cut through the darkness and across the park towards home. "Losing her marbles, I guess." And his whisper was snatched away from his lips by the wind that circled him.

Screeeeech! Screeeeech! Screeeeech!

Michael stopped. The sound had been sudden. Had it been a wail? The sound of an animal close by? A tiger, perhaps? Michael peered over the collar of his blazer. The sound came again. A screeching sound, like an animal in pain.

There are tigers! The voice whispered in his ear, and it was his grandmother's.

"There ain't no tigers!" Michael said aloud.

The sound came again – like fingernails being dragged across ice.

"Why did Nan have to try and scare me like that?" Michael groaned, his heart racing behind his chest like a triphammer. Then through the driving rain, Michael saw what it was that was making the noise.

The swings swung back and forth in the wind as if being pushed by the ghosts of children who had come back from their graves to have one last night of fun in the park.

"I knew there were no tigers," Michael laughed at himself. Pulling his blazer tight, he set off again towards home and the underpass.

However hard he fought the urge, Michael couldn't help but quicken his step. It was as if he no longer had control over his legs. At first his stride got longer, swallowing up the pavement in front of him like a ravenous animal. Then his pace got faster, a slow trot at first – then a quick jog – until his legs were pin-wheeling beneath him like propellers. Then he was racing through the evening streets, away from the swings in the park, but most of all from his grandmother's rasping voice and her warning of tigers.

Michael reached the path that led home. He lent forward and sucked mouthfuls of air into his burning lungs. He buried his fingers deep into the flesh beneath his ribcage and tried to ease the stitch that smouldered inside him like a hot poker. Michael knew that just on the other side of the hill that stood before him like an ogre was his house, warm, dry and safe.

Michael eyed the hill before him, black, wet, and slippery. He could climb it, but he felt exhausted, damp, and cold. Rain ran down the hill in tiny rivulets and he could picture himself slipping, tumbling over and over in the mud and breaking an arm, or worse, a leg. He thought of the cup-tie he was playing in that weekend and didn't want to risk an injury before match day.

There was another option. Michael didn't have to risk climbing over the hill – he could go underneath it – he could take the underpass. Michael looked at the entrance to the underpass and it was dark and wide like the jaws of a giant beast – a tiger's jaws.

There are tigers beneath the underpass! His grandmother's voice croaked in his ear again.

Forcing the sound of her voice away, Michael walked towards the entrance. He stood within its concrete jaws and the smell of urine, vomit, and stale cannabis smoke wafted under his nose and made him feel sick. Placing one foot in front of the other, he stepped inside. Only minutes ago, his feet had been unable to stop moving – whispering above the rain-soaked pavement. But now they felt like lumps of lead disappearing into quicksand. Michael forced himself onwards.

There are tigers... his Nan's voice started up again.

"Go away, will ya!" Michael hissed at the voice inside his head.

"There ain't no tigers here!"

The underpass was lit with a strip of fluorescent lights, but most had been smashed by vandals, leaving pools of murky light every few yards. The tiled walls had been decorated with graffiti. Slogans and symbols had been painted. Michael could see a red line of paint that had been sprayed from a can in an arc across the wall of the underpass. He looked at it, and in the dim light of the underpass he thought that the paint could have been blood, sprayed from the throat of someone attacked by a ti...

Then there were shadows in the corner of his eye, and Michael turned away from the paint...

Blood? and peered into the gloom.

"Who's there?" Michael called out, his voice echoing off the underpass walls like drum beats.

Silence.

"Is anyone there?" he called again.

Silence.

Screwing up his eyes, Michael strained to see what was making the shadows ahead of him. They were tall, pointed, and moved slowly towards him. The shadows were far too tall to be tigers and a nervous laugh escaped him as he thought of how stupid he was being.

"The only tigers down here are the members of that gang," he assured himself.

The shadows came closer.

"What do you want?" Michael called out.

Closer still.

"Look, if you think you're gonna rob a mobile from me, you're outta luck. I don't even own a phone."

Closer.

"Look, I'm just on my way home," Michael said, and his voice sounded high-pitched and broken. He felt his innards tighten, and his stomach made an odd gargling sound like acid sloshing around in a bucket. "I don't want any trouble. I just want to go home."

In the darkness, inches ahead of him, six bright orange lights appeared. They glowed like hot coals on a roaring fire. Michael stared at them. At first he couldn't figure out what they were. They blinked on and off like the indicators on a car. Then as they came nearer, he realised with dread what they were.

The eyes stared at him from the darkness. Three sets of blazing orange eyes.

But what or who would have orange eyes? Michael screamed inside as he stumbled backwards down the underpass.

There are... his grandmother's voice began again in his ear.

"Shut up! Shut up! Shut up, Nan!" Michael screeched, covering his ears with his hands. "There ain't no..."

The last of his sentence was drowned out by a deafening snarling sound. The noise came at him like a wave and knocked him from his feet in a rush of hot air. Michael slammed into the ground, forcing the air from his lungs. The shadows before him began to change shape, growing longer and sleeker-looking. They sauntered towards him, powerful but graceful.

Michael tried to scream, but the only noise that came from his throat was a gagging sound. He didn't even scream as the giant orange and black striped paw sprung from the darkness and opened his chest. Michael looked down in disbelief at the gaping crimson hole. He then looked up into the tiger's face. For a moment he thought that the creature looked beautiful with its white and orange muzzle. Its whiskers glinted like lengths of silver thread in the murky light of the underpass. Then that glimpse of beauty was gone. The tiger opened his powerful jaws revealing rows of jagged teeth. Michael could feel the heat of the tiger's breath against his cheek and the smell of dead things and flesh wafting from its slobbering tongue. Then that beautiful white muzzle turned red – brilliant red - as the tiger buried its face into Michael's chest.

There are tigers beneath that underpass, Michael heard his grandmother whisper in his ear one last time.

Ratbag

Frannie Lauderdale walked slowly down the long corridor. The echoey snap of her heels on the stone floor made a chattering sound like a woman's teeth rattling together in the cold. Frannie suddenly stopped short, and a thin gasp of surprise slipped from between her lips as a sudden streak of purple lightning streaked the dark sky outside. A coating of luminous colours splashed Frannie's face as her grey eyes grew wide with fright. She hastened her step.

Dougie Nicholson stepped from the shadows several yards behind Frannie, who he had been following. He paused for a moment as the girl ahead stopped, as the lightning raged in anger outside again. Dougie heard her sudden gasp as it slipped back over her shoulder towards him. The school corridor flashed with a sudden burst of light and his face looked as if it had been carved from alabaster. The flash of light disappeared as quickly as it had come, and the girl started to move on towards the chapel at a faster pace.

Dougie followed, not because he wanted to hurt her – but because he was in love with Frannie. He loved everything about her and he was sure that he was the only boy at St. Stephen's High School who did. The other boys and all of the girls, in fact, didn't like her because she was different. She came from a family that was very poor, and she dressed from the flea market and some said that she smelt real bad. But there was something else that made her different - Frannie had one big, fat juicy secret. A secret – a dark secret – which Dougie knew nothing about. A secret he had to discover for himself. Dougie had only been at St. Stephen's High School a month, and in that time he had made several friends – who, if he were being honest with himself, he didn't like none too much. He had been placed in detention three times for failing to hand in homework on time, and had fallen in love with the school Ratbag.

So that's why he was following her today, to discover her secret, which kept him from sleeping at night. The other kids on the schoolyard had hinted many times that the secret had something to do with what she carried in the brown paper bag that she carried clutched to her swelling chest. But Dougie wondered if the stories about this dark secret were not just wicked lies, rumours spread about Frannie because she was different. Dougie knew that if there wasn't any gossip to spread, then people usually made up their own. That's what Dougie needed to find out – did Frannie really have a dark and terrible secret?

Frannie bobbed up and down as she moved towards the chapel, a quiet place where she could be alone. Her fountain of rich, auburn hair cascaded down her back like lava. Her two thin arms hung from the sleeves of her grubby T-shirt. Her checked skirt, held together at the waist with a safety pin, swished about her knees. Her legs were creamy in colour and slipped away into a pair of scuffed brown shoes. As she made her way down the corridor, she would pause suddenly as the lightning continued to split the sky in two on the other side of the stained-glass windows. Rain spattered the windows, which loomed up on her left every few feet. Frannie would sometimes disappear in the gloominess and then reappear when she passed one of those windows. Purple flashes of light almost seemed to soak her up.

Careful not to be seen by her, Dougie followed at a safe distance, loving the sudden glimpses he got of her. Every time she halted, he would duck into the shadows, just in case she stole a quick glance back over her shoulder. But he didn't really need to bother. His school uniform was all black; the only pale garment was his face.

Her scuffed shoes continued to make a snap-slap sound on the cold stone floor, and in the flashes of light, he thought she looked beautiful and he couldn't understand the cruel comments that the other kids made about her. He had often brushed deliberately against her in the corridor, hoping that she would lift her head and notice him, but she never did. But when he was close to her like that, her hair and skin had smelt of soap. The end of the corridor loomed ahead.

Frannie disappeared to her right with a quick swish of her flowing hair. The snap-slap of her worn-down heels slowly ebbed away as she bobbed into the chapel. She paused by the open doorway, and with a flick of her right wrist, she dipped her doll-like fingers into the small font fastened to the chapel wall. She made the sign if the cross by touching her forehead and chest, then walked slowly into the dimly-lit chapel.

Dougie ducked right and stopped flat against the wall as he watched Frannie moved down the threadbare carpet that lined the floor between the rows of seats. The chapel was barely lit by a cluster of slow burning candles in the corner. Dougie watched his love as she bobbed down the aisle. Once he was sure that he wasn't going to be seen by her, Dougie stepped from the safety of the shadows. But almost at once he was forced to hide in them again, as Frannie came to a sudden halt ahead of him. Dougie spied on her, his chest rising with laboured, anxious breaths. Plumes of air escaped from his mouth in wispy clouds and disappeared into the freezing cold chapel.

Frannie had stopped by the end of a pew. Then, as if not believing what he was seeing, Frannie appeared to be sinking into the ground. Dougie screwed his eyes almost shut as he peered into the darkness. But to his relief, he could see she was only genuflecting in front of the huge crucifix which hung on the wall. Frannie stayed on her knees, her hair looking as if it were on fire as it reflected back the spooky candlelight. With that brown paper bag clutched to her chest, Frannie crawled between the rows of pews. It was as if she disappeared in stages, first her head, then shoulders, upper body, bottom, legs, then last of all, her feet. Dougie frowned as he watched her hide between the pews.

He waited for just a few seconds, then left the coldness of the shadows and followed the path Frannie had taken down the centre of the chapel. The white stone walls almost seemed to come alive as the candlelight flickered off them in a sudden draught. Dougie shivered, his skin over run with gooseflesh. A steady hiss of rain could be heard from overhead as it drummed against the rickety roof. Dougie's trainers whispered on the carpet with each step he took nearer to Frannie as she sheltered in her hiding place.

He could see the two pews that she had crawled between just ahead. As he got nearer, he walked on tiptoe. He didn't want to make a sound. Dougie didn't want to disturb Frannie if he were to discover her big, fat, juicy secret. He slowed then stopped, just behind the pew where Frannie had performed her disappearing act. Lowering himself onto his hands and knees, Dougie crawled into the gap between the pews. He had gone a short distance, when he stopped to listen. Up ahead, on the other side of the pew, he heard a rustling sound, then a frantic squealing noise. With his heart racing in his ears, he knew that he was just inches away from discovering Frannie's secret.

Dougie drew level with her on the opposite side of the pew. The rustling sound came again, and it sounded as if someone or something were struggling. Drawing a deep breath, Dougie waited and waited and waited, then suddenly popped his head up and peered over the top of the pew. He looked down and he shoved a fist into his mouth to stifle a scream.

Frannie sat with her legs drawn up to her chest, back arched as she chewed away at a sandwich. But the sandwich looked as if it were moving – *squirming* – somehow. Between the two thick white slices of bread which Frannie had sunk her teeth into, something fat, black and hairy wriggled between the slices. Then, he saw it – something pink, thin, and long, swishing frantically from side to side. It was a tail – a rat's tail. He made a gaging noise in the back of his throat, and Frannie heard it. Snapping her head around, she looked up at Dougie. But instead of looking shocked at finding him there, she just smiled sweetly at him, black clumps of wiry black fur sticking out from between her teeth.

Then, cocking an eyebrow, she held out her hand and offered him the half-eaten sandwich. Dougie smiled back at

Frannie, and stretching out his hand, he plucked the writhing sandwich from her and took a bite.

Paisley End

Shane Cole sat behind the wheel of his old Ford truck. The windscreen wipers squeaked back and forth furiously as they tried to drive off the falling rain. The truck rattled and shook as it moved slowly down the winding country lanes. Dark clouds moved across the leafy sky. Bluish–mauve sparks of lightning flashed from behind the clouds and lit up the sky like a crazy firework display. Thunder sounded as if a thousand iron balls were being rolled across the floors of heaven. Rain fell heavier in long, sparkling streaks. Mud spattered up off the road and freckled the bumper, mud-guards, and sides of the truck, yet it rumbled on. Fields stretched out on either side of the road, and they looked dull and grey through the rain.

Shane sat with his back hunched over the steering wheel, concentrating hard as he guided the truck around the tight bends in the road. The wind howled and it almost seemed to whisper as it entwined itself around the trees and raced across the open fields. It sounded like a thousand voices moaning all at once. Crows squawked as they fluttered up from the cornfields and took shelter beneath the leaves of the trees.

The truck slowed, listed to the right, sloshed through a giant ditch, then carried on. Shane took one hand from the wheel and rubbed the back of it against the mist-covered windscreen. Once he had made a clearing, he gasped with surprise on seeing a figure step from the side of the road up ahead. The figure made a fist and waved its thumb back and forth in the air. As Shane pushed the truck on through the storm, he could see that the figure was in fact a bedraggled looking man. He wore only a grubby T-shirt, blue jeans, trainers, and had a duffle bag thrown over his shoulder.

Shane glanced up at the bruised and battered sky, and although half of him wanted drive straight on, the other half knew that he had to stop. The man looked soaked through. Shane slowed the truck to a juddering halt. He slid across the seat and opened the passenger door.

"Hey, son, where you heading?" Shane shouted over the sound of the screeching wind.

The man was much younger than Shane. He couldn't have been any older than twenty-two or twenty-three. Rain dripped from his long, jet-black hair and onto his face and clothes. His face was pale, and his sea-green eyes stared out of two sunken sockets.

"Where you going?" Shane yelled again.

"Paisley End. Going anywhere near?" the man asked.

"Near enough," Shane told him. "Jump in."

Shane offered the stranger a friendly smile and slid back across the seat. The man got in and pulled the door shut. Shane drove on.

"Bitter out there?" Shane asked, knowing it to be a dumb question but conversations usually started with talk of the weather.

"You bet, its freezing," the younger man said, rubbing his arms and shivering.

Shane rubbed the windscreen with the back of his hand again, then settled back into his seat. "I didn't catch your name," he said.

"Jon. Jon Cooke," the man replied. "Yours?"

"Shane Cole. It's nice to meet you, Jon," he said back.

They sat in an uncomfortable silence for a moment, but Shane soon broke it. "You're frozen right through. Take a look in the back and you'll find my coat. Put it on if you'd like."

"Thanks," Jon said, reaching into the rear of the truck. He rummaged through some old newspapers, books, and fishing gear until he found Shane's coat. It was khaki and expensive. Jon put it on and found that it was way too big for him, so he snuggled down into it and blew warm breath across his fingers.

"Feeling better?" Shane asked him.

"Yes, much better, thanks."

"Good. You looked like death warmed up standing along the roadside," Shane remarked.

"I'd been waiting for a while. You don't get much traffic out this way, it's pretty remote," Jon said, rubbing his hands together.

"That's true," Shane said. "If you don't mind me asking – why are you going to Paisley End?"

"For some peace and quiet," Jon told him.

"You'll get it there," Shane said. "I've never been, but heard rumours that it's kind of dead there – you know, people keep themselves to themselves. They don't welcome strangers."

"If I'm to be honest, I got myself into a bit of trouble back home, so I'm kind of hiding for a while," Jon explained.

"Trouble?" Shane asked, cocking an eyebrow at him. "With the law?"

"No, nothing like that," Jon said. "Girl trouble. Trying to keep away from her father. He's really pissed at me. Besides, I'm a musician. I play the flute."

"Any good?" Shane asked.

"Not bad," Jon said. "I'm self-taught. Comes kinda natural, I guess. I'm planning on writing some music down here. You know, a bit of fresh air, beautiful scenery, peace and quiet – that sort of thing."

"You'll get plenty of peace and quiet in Paisley End," Shane commented. "It's pretty much a dead-end sorta place."

"Where are you going?" Jon asked, pulling the coat about him.

"A place called Weather Beach," Shane said. "I turn off about two or so miles before Paisley End. My daughter has a place there. Great for fishing."

The truck rumbled on through the rain and the wind, Shane and Jon chatting all the way. After about an hour and with no let-up in the bad weather, Shane pulled over.

"This is as far as I go," Shane said.

"I appreciate the lift," Jon smiled, pushing the door open against the wind.

"Don't mention it," Shane said, then added, "It's none of my business, but maybe after you found what you're looking for in Paisley End, you should maybe go home to that girl you got into trouble with. It's hard bringing up a kid on your own, I should know."

"I'll think about it," Jon said. He closed the door to the truck, and hoisting his duffle bag over his shoulder, he set off in the direction of Paisley End and the dull day gradually turned into night.

Shane stepped on the accelerator and drove the truck towards Weather Beach. He looked forward to seeing his daughter again, and the fishing, of course. With more than an hour or so of driving left to go, and with his companion gone, Shane lent forward, opened the glove box and rummaged around for a cigarette. He'd promised his daughter that he'd quit, but he had cut down. Unable to find a packet, and keeping one eye on the road ahead, he swung his arm over the back of his seat and felt for his coat. It wasn't there and he suddenly remembered he had lent it to Jon.

"For crying out loud," Shane cursed, remembering that his wallet, credit cards, and cigarettes were in the pockets of the coat, he slammed on the brakes. Reversing back up the road, which was little more than a dirt track, Shane reached the point where he had last seen Jon walking away into the distance. Knowing that it had been little more than ten minutes since Jon had gotten out of the truck, Shane sped towards Paisley End, hoping that he would soon catch up with him and his coat.

The truck rattled and bobbed over the rain-swollen ditches and puddles, and after twenty minutes or more, he was surprised that he hadn't caught up with Jon. He pushed the truck onwards. Then ahead, Shane saw a sign that read, *Welcome to Paisley End*. Stopping the truck, Shane rubbed the windscreen with the back of his hand again and peered out. Beneath the welcome sign, someone had written, *Children Beware*.

Not knowing what to make of the sign, Shane paused. Did he really want to go on? But his jacket was there. So easing his truck into gear, he headed into town. Just like the other roads, they were little more than lanes, with overgrown hedges on either side. The road was uneven, and Shane bounced around in his seat as he drove on. But there was still no sign of Jon Cooke.

Up ahead, Shane could see lights twinkling in the distance in the falling rain. He suddenly felt glad that he was finally reaching some kind of civilisation. Houses, shops, and people, he hoped. Shane swung the truck onto the first tarmacked road that he had seen in hours. He raced towards the lights in the distance. As he drew nearer to them, he could see that it was a petrol station and roadside café that he was heading towards.

Shane slowed the truck and veered into the car park and got out. With his head low and shoulders hunched forward, he ran towards the café, as the rain lashed down all around him. The café was shabby-looking, the roof bowed inwards, and the brickwork was cracked and moss-ridden. The windows looked dirty, and the curtains had a yellow tinge to them. Shane pushed the door open and stepped out of the rain. The café was dimly-lit, and people sat huddled around small tables. Seeing him enter, they all looked up at once and fixed him with an unfriendly stare. It was as Shane looked around the room at them, he noticed that their faces were deathly white, which spoke of unhappiness and sorrow. They eyes were red-rimmed, bloodshot, and each of them looked as if they recently spent many hours crying.

Breaking their unfriendly stares, Shane shook the rain from his grey hair and made his way to the counter, which doubled as a bar. Behind it slouched a withered old man. His face was a mass of wrinkles. His eyes, just like the others, were almost puffed closed. As he watched Shane approach, the old man pulled a cloth from his pocket and began to wipe down the counter. He worked, but his heart wasn't in it. Shane stopped in front of the coffee-stained bar.

"Can I help you?" the old man asked, and Shane couldn't help but notice that his voice was riddled with suspicion.

"I hope so," Shane said right back.

"Tea? Coffee? Or something stronger?" the old man asked.

"No, nothing, thanks. I'm fine," Shane told him. "I would just like some information." But with the feeling that all those eyes were boring into him, he just wanted to run from the café and get right back in his truck and out of town.

"What sort?" the old man snapped.

"Has a young man passed this way in the last hour or so?" Shane asked.

The old man made no reply and went back to cleaning the counter. Shane tried again. "He was in his early twenties, was wearing a khaki coat and carrying a duffle bag over his shoulder."

The old man turned his back on Shane and started to busy himself by cleaning some cups.

"His name was Jon Cooke," Shane started up again. "Do you know..."

Before he'd had a chance to finish his sentence, a woman sitting behind him made a screeching sound, as if she had a chicken bone stuck in the back of her throat. She then burst into a fit of hysterics and ran sobbing from the café. Others jumped up from their tables, sending cups, plates, knives, and forks clattering to the floor. They ran from the café, weeping and moaning.

The old man wheeled around at Shane, and with their faces just inches apart, he hissed, "If you're not going to stop for refreshments, *get out!*"

Shane's face drained of all colour, and his heart began to thump in his chest, but still he persisted. "Have you seen him? That's all I want to know and then I will be gone."

The villagers continued to brush past Shane as they headed towards the door and fled into the storm, and he couldn't understand why. The old man fixed his milky-looking eyes on Shane's.

"Okay, mister," he sneered. "I'll tell you all about Jon Cooke. He came into town about three months ago, and just as you say, he carried a duffle bag over his shoulder. But he had something else. A flute. It was the strangest thing I had ever seen. Not like your everyday flute. This was black and looked as if it was made of some kinda ancient ivory. He took to

177

standing on the street corners, playing his flute. Didn't matter what the weather – he was always there, that flute between his lips. The music that came from it was like nothing I'd heard before – it sounded like a thousand children crying. The children would gather around him – as if they were in a trance. Us adults didn't like it one little bit, so we told him to clear out of town. He did, but he returned, several nights later," the old man explained, and as he did, his voice no longer sounded angry, but full of despair.

"Jon Cooke," he continued, with tears beginning to well in his eyes, "hidden by the night and the shadows of the trees, played his flute while the adults slept. But the music stirred the children from their sleep. Like zombies, they crept from their beds and followed Cooke across the fields and up into the hills. They haven't been seen again, not one of them."

The old man stopped, pulled a snot-ridden hanky from his pocket, and wiped his lips, then brow. "The following day, the men from the village, me included, set off in pursuit of Cooke. We found him, but none of the children he had led away into the night. We punished him for what he had done – we punished him real bad – so he could never steal another child again. We hurt him so bad that you couldn't have seen him today – that would be impossible," he whispered, then broke into a sinister cackle of laughter. Then, sounding as if had phlegm wrapped around his tonsils, he leaned over the counter and hissed, "Now get out."

Feeling so confused by what he had just heard, Shane wanted to question the old man further. But before he'd had the chance to saying at all, the owner had gone to the door, opened it and turned the sign over to CLOSED. Knowing that his presence was no longer wanted, if it ever had been, Shane left the café and headed back to his truck.

Once inside and away from the café and its odd owner and customers, gooseflesh crawled up Shane's back and made the hairs at the nape of his neck prickle. No longer interested in ever seeing his coat again, he started up his truck and raced back up the road and out of town. As Paisley End disappeared behind him, Shane slowed the truck down. Then, as he neared the edge of town and the welcome sign, he slammed on the brakes. Shane lurched forward in his seat and stared out into the dark and rain; there was something caught in the glare of his headlights. With his mouth open and his heart struggling to find a beat, Shane slowly opened the truck door and stepped out. He climbed over a low stone wall and into a field and looked up at the tree which sat alone, away from the others. It was leafless and its black branches reached up into the sky like deformed limbs. Its trunk was thick and gnarled-looking, and tied to it with rope, was Jon Cooke.

Unable to draw breath, Shane stumbled over the uneven ground as he made his way towards the tree. Standing before it, he could see that the body of Jon Cooke had already started to decompose, as if he had been left there to rot for several weeks already. Crows squawked and beat their ragged wings as they fluttered away from the branches overhead. Shane looked at the body of Jon Cooke and gagged at the sight of the maggots which crawled from his empty eye sockets. One eye hung from its socket on a sinewy cord, looking like a yo-yo made of red flesh. His tongue hung like a giant black worm from a jagged tear in his cheek. His mouth was open in an insane looking grin, and his teeth glistened in the light from the truck's headlights.

But it wasn't the sight of Jon Cooke's decomposed body which made Shane's blood feel like ice in his veins. It was the fact that Jon Cooke was wearing his coat. Daring to step closer to the body, Shane noticed something black and pointed sticking out from his coat pocket. Reaching out, Shane plucked the odd-looking flute from his coat. It felt weightless in his hands. Then, as if unable to resist the urge, he placed the flute to his lips and blew gently into it.

As Shane made his way back to his truck in that awful storm, playing the flute as he went, he knew that the old man from the café had been right, the music which came from it did sound like a thousand children crying.

A Story

Jim Chambers sat with his arse wedged into the narrow chair, striking the keys on the typewriter that squatted before him. The metal keys snapped back and forth, leaving their design behind on the crisp, white paper. His words and thoughts appeared in neat rows. The letter 'A' key was missing, snapped off years before so he would have to spend time hand writing in all the missing letter 'A's to his story once he had finished.

Beads of sweat lined Jim's young face as his tongue flicked from the corner of his mouth while he concentrated on his writing. He had to complete his story, not only for himself, but for her. His creative writing teacher's greed for his stories was unending. She would take each one in her gnarled hands and smile thankfully, like a drunk who is handed another drink. Jim was secretly pleased that someone relished his tales of horror and fantasy, where people lived shrouded in darkness, surviving the blood-foaming jaws of the creatures that he created. Sometimes they didn't always survive. He liked the power that gave him.

But Jim thought it strange that someone like his teacher should love his stories so much. He guessed that Ms. Mitchell was in her late sixties and was a dead ringer for Miss Marple. How could someone who shuffled around with a shawl thrown over her shoulders, and who had glasses hanging from the tip of her nose give a second thought to such revolting tales? But did it really matter? He was glad he had one fan, even if wasn't his girlfriend, Wendy. Wendy didn't care for his stories at all. So with his creative writing teacher at the forefront of his mind, he continued to tap out his story...

...the crackling noise which could be heard beneath the woman's blouse was sickening to hear. The folds of her blouse moved restlessly. She brought her worn hands to her blouse and ripped it in two, the buttons popping free and clinking onto the floor. Her saggy breasts writhed and twitched, becoming transparent, revealing the membranes that lay just beneath her aged skin. Blue veins circled her chest, the skin thinning out across her shoulders, up her neck and face.

Dark lines lay etched about the corners of her mouth. Her skin began to fade and her yellow-stained teeth and lolling tongue became visible through her cheek. Her forehead became a window, its view a pulsating brain. She unfastened her skirt and it whispered to the floor. She pulled at her black tights with pulsating hands until she was free of them. Her stomach and bowels could be seen through her invisible skin. The smell of rotting and undigested food was rich and pungent on the dry air.

The woman fell to the floor, landing on her hands and knees. The air began to fill with a ripping sound as her shoulder blades, spine, and hands began to stretch out of shape, giving her the appearance of a squat, four-legged animal. She began to crack and blister as stiff, black hair oozed out of her. Her bloodless lips stretched open as a twitching snout appeared. Twisted, blade-like teeth protruded through her swelling gums, sending blood forth in a black gush which swung from her whiskered chin.

Her gnarled fingers buckled and became claws as her knuckles shattered. The woman's body was to undergo one final change before her metamorphosis was complete. The bottom of her raised spine exploded outwards. Through the gaping hole in her back appeared a slender pink tail which glistened and licked back and forth in the air, blind to what lay around it.

The huge black rat sprang off into the night on its strong back legs.

Jim snatched the sheet from his typewriter and reread his tale, the corners of his youthful mouth turning up in delight as he did so. He knew she would love this one.

He slouched like a drunk against the wall opposite his classroom. Some of Jim's classmates had already filed into the room, but he wasn't ready to start his first lesson of the day without first seeing Wendy. His bag lay at his feet and he regarded it carefully. Inside laid his latest story. His pallor was a washed-out grey, apart from the purple rings of tiredness that lay beneath his eyes. Jim had sat up late correcting his tale, hand-writing in all the missing 'A's and trying to get it perfect in every way before submitting it to Ms. Mitchell. He was pleased with the final result.

Jim glanced to his right and smiled at the sight of Wendy approaching from down the hall. She bobbed as she came, her shoes snapping off the tiled floor. Jim met her halfway and they kissed. Her hair was fair and it shone beneath the glare of the fluorescent lights. Her eyes were a warm hazel, her mouth a pink smile.

"You look like shit," she told him. "What time did you hit the sack last night?"

"Not until late, and thanks for the compliment," he half-smiled.

"You know what I mean," she said, and kissed him again on the cheek.

"I didn't get to bed until the early hours," he started, but before he could finish, Wendy was squeezing his side.

"I hope you were alone," she teased.

Jim chuckled and pulled away. "Well it was so hard to resist her, but she was..."

Wendy tweaked him again.

He threw his arms in the air and cried, "I give in. I was writing last night – honest."

Wendy let him be and gave a satisfied smile. "I believe you. What were you writing? Something pleasant, I hope."

"You know me better than that," and a fat grin spread across his face.

"I might have known. You and your ghouls," she laughed.

Then looking at her, Jim said, "Well you know who I base them on, don't you?" He spoke in a teasing way.

Wendy placed her hands on her hips and said, "If you mean me, Jim Chambers, then you're in trouble!"

"Now, I didn't say you – did I? But come to mention it," he winked at her and scratched his chin.

Wendy had started to tickle him again, when they were both interrupted.

"Excuse me, Chambers, but you do have a lesson to attend," a voice said from behind them.

They both froze, then turned their heads in the direction of the soft sounding voice. Jim didn't have to see her lined face, greying hair, and piercing eyes to know that it was Ms. Mitchell who had spoken. He stepped away from Wendy, blood burning in his cheeks.

"I'm sorry, Ms. Mitchell," he said, picking up his bag. As he thought of the story inside, he smiled.

"Don't be sorry," Ms. Mitchell said. "I can remember what it was like to be in love once."

Both Jim and Wendy flushed scarlet again, wondering if Ms. Mitchell wasn't actually taking some pleasure in embarrassing them. The old woman stepped back into the classroom. Jim skipped quickly over to Wendy. They kissed, and Jim told her to wait for him on the yard after lesson. Wendy nodded, hoping that the time between now and then would pass quickly. She disappeared up the corridor and Jim turned and entered the classroom.

Ms. Mitchell smiled with pleasure as Jim laid the story in her liver-spotted hands. She took it gratefully. "Another tale. How exciting," she breathed and stroked the pages. "James, I'll read it this very lesson. Thank you." She turned and moved slowly towards her desk, eyes fixed on his manuscript.

Jim went to his own seat, feeling pleased.

Ms. Mitchell set some work for the class, then buried her nose in the story she clutched in her hands. Her eyes rolled back and forth as they soaked up the words Jim had written. He sat and watched her read over the lip of his workbook. Jim liked to study her expressions which fell across her face as she read his stories. But today something was wrong. Ms. Mitchell didn't have a look of pleasure on her face, but a look of anger.

The lesson passed. The class milled from the room on her command and she requested that Jim should stay behind as he always did when she was in possession of one of his stories.

"Not you," she whispered, hooking one of her fingers and beckoning him forward.

Jim gathered his books together and strolled to the front of the classroom. "What did you think of my story, Ms. Mitchell?" He shifted from foot to foot.

"It was very good, as they always are," she said, her eyes fixed on his. "You have quite a talent."

Ms. Mitchell moved to the classroom door, shut it tight, then turned the key in the lock. Taking hold of the key, she turned to look at Jim. She poked her grey-looking tongue out, placed the key on it, then swallowed. Jim watched the lines on her neck ripple as the key passed down her throat. With his stomach beginning to tighten and his heart racing, he watched his teacher shuffle back across the classroom towards him.

"Tell me, James," she whispered. "How did you know? How did you ever find out?"

"Find out about what?" Jim asked, he frowned with a nervous smile.

"Me," she suddenly snarled.

Jim stood gawping at her, his eyes fat and round with fear. The folds in her pastel blouse began to move as her flesh began to change shape beneath it. The change from woman to rat took just seconds. Before Jim had even had the chance to truly understand what had happened, a set of razor-sharp teeth were ripping at his throat.

Wendy stood on the yard, a chilly wind tugging at her hair, as she waited and waited and waited...

'Dead Statues'

Kiera Hudson Series Two Book Three Coming Soon!

'Cowgirls & Vampires' - Out Now!

More books by Tim O'Rourke
Vampire Shift (Kiera Hudson Series 1) Book 1
Vampire Wake (Kiera Hudson Series 1) Book 2
Vampire Hunt (Kiera Hudson Series 1) Book 3
Vampire Breed (Kiera Hudson Series 1) Book 4
Wolf House (Kiera Hudson Series 1) Book 4.5
Vampire Hollows (Kiera Hudson Series 1) Book 5
Dead Flesh (Kiera Hudson Series 2) Book 1
Dead Night (Kiera Hudson Series 2) Book 1.5
Dead Angels (Kiera Hudson Series 2) Book 2
Cowgirls & Vampires (Samantha Carter Series) Book 1
Black Hill Farm (Book 1)
Black Hill Farm: Andy's Diary (Book 2)
Doorways (Book 1)

About the author
Working away in the dead of night, Tim has written many short stories, plays and novels. Tim is the author of the bestselling 'Kiera Hudson Series', the two paranormal romance books entitled 'Black Hill Farm' and the 'Doorways' Trilogy.
Tim is currently working on a new series called 'Cowgirls & Vampires'. The first book is now available.
Tim's interests other than writing, include watching South Park, Vampire Diaries, True Blood and listening to Pitbull, LMFAO, Jennifer Lopez, David Guetta, Bruno Mars, Rihanna and Adele. Tim is never happier than when reading The Twilight Series, Vampire Diaries and writing his own Vampire series 'Kiera Hudson' and 'Cowgirls & Vampires'.
Don't be shy, feel free to contact Tim, he would love to hear from you.
Email: Ravenwoodgreys@aol.com Website: www.Ravenwoodgreys.com

9 781478 377368